CHAPLAIN

A NOVELLA OF EXTREME TERROR

DAVID W.
COONS JR

Printed in the United States of America

First Printing, 2016

ISBN-13: 978-1523888696
ISBN-10: 1523888695

MEGMAR Entertainment
  c/o DWC Publishing
P.O. Box 928584
San Diego, CA 92192

https://www.facebook.com/davidcoonsauthor

ALSO BY DAVID W COONS JR

SHORTS

BY THE HOUR: A HORRIFIC NOVELETTE

NOVELS

SIXTEEN YEARS AGO (coming 2016)

August 23rd, 1893

I don't have much time. Even now your mother conspires against me. She will be bringing them here soon. Bringing them to take me away and lock me up in a cell, where they will undoubtedly toss the key away into some dark nether region, never to be found again.

All because I trusted her. I trusted her with my tale. The tale that I have held with me for so many years, never uttering to another living soul. Since I may never see another sunrise, nor will I be able to converse with you once you are of an age to understand my words, I am hurriedly recording them here; in this journal that has sat blank for far too many years.

I knew that it was not the right thing to do in telling her. I *had* to, though. It was the only choice at the time to save my marriage. We were married merely four years before; at a time when I thought I had left the past behind for good.

When I first met her - her smile burned bright, her eyes held the promise of a heaven I had never dared to know - over five years had passed since the last time the evil had plagued me. I thought I was safe. Then, like a storm over the plains, the evil returned without warning. These last few weeks, things have been bad. Things that have caused her to doubt my sanity. Things that have caused her to doubt *me*.

Times were trying and she was scared. I do not blame her – I *cannot* blame her – for that. I'm sure in her mind, I had, at best, revealed myself to be a blubbering lunatic. At worst, a monster. My story was the only hope I held to change that belief.

It did not.

If anything, it further convinced her of my insanity. My depravity. I could not convince her otherwise and she has since become a most foul and bitter woman towards me in recourse to the fear that I had wrought. Again, I cannot blame her, but my anger towards her seethes, nonetheless.

Perhaps, even that can be blamed upon the evil feeding on me.

So, son, I implore you to read these words carefully. Read them and take them how they are intended...as a warning. Heed my cautionary tale and forever avoid following in the footsteps of your old man. Live your life whole, and let the evil lie still in the past.

July 3rd, 1863

My story starts on a mild summer morning. The sun burned hot, but a steady breeze countered it. It was the kind of day where one could sit in the shade of tree and read a good book, or just enjoy the many splendors that nature had to offer.

Except, on that particular day, the thunderous roar of gunfire kept coherent thought from forming and the gun smoke was of such a thickness that every breath felt labored.

My father and I had arrived on June 30th to a little hamlet in the land of William Penn. I'm sure you will know the name from your schoolmarms when you reach a learning age. The town was named Gettysburg, and that name would forevermore be synonymous with the bloodshed that soaked the grounds red over the course of three fateful days in early July.

Dawn had brought with it the third straight day of the fighting. The aforementioned gunfire accompanied by the screams of fifty thousand dying men easily intruded on us through the thin, wooden walls of the barn that we were holed up in. Even the rare break in the aural horrors from outside the walls failed to bring true silence. Those scattered moments were filled with the whimpering of the nearly eighty souls bunkered down with us. Mostly women and children; very few men of a fighting age.

I was a mere boy just shy of my tenth birthday and one would think me as scared as the huddled masses which vilified the tight space with their unwashed bodies. I tell you the opposite was true. I was not scared on that day, nor the two prior.

I was intrigued.

I had followed the Great War since its inception. The one the southern rebels had inconceivably dubbed "The War of Northern Aggression". I had only seen seven years of life when those first shots were fired at Fort Sumter, but those shots had awaken in me a hunger for the curiosities of war. Every time I would see the soldiers marching through our town, I tried asking them questions about the war. What was it like? How many have been killed? Why I had such a fascination with brother killing brother I do not know to this day, but there was no arguing that my desires for knowledge on the matter were insatiable.

My father and I had traveled to Gettysburg on what was supposed to be a quick a business trip. Father had let me tag along only because I had been a pest in his ear about it since the day that I had first learned of it. I knew that the war had affected many areas near there, and I had hoped to visit some of the nearby battlefields. Though, truthfully, I had no notion that the bloodiest battle of the entire war would spring up so close to our destination as to consume it whole.

"Father, I have to pee," I begged, making a show of jumping up and down with my hands tucked between my legs.

"You sure you can't hold it? That soldier that came by a bit ago informed us that the battle has turned. The Union is winning this battle now. God-willing, it should all be over soon enough."

Which is exactly the reason that I chose that time to make my move.

"No! I have to go now!" I prodded, injecting my tone with the most perturbing juvenile squeal I could muster. My father sighed and offered to walk me to the outhouse one building over.

Of course, that wasn't going to work for me.

"That's okay, Father. Jeremiah has to go, too. He says he'll watch out for me."

Jeremiah was a boy that I had met over those days in the barn. He was fourteen and the adults would often trust him to accompany the younger children to the outhouse.

What they didn't know was that he was a war fanatic like myself. He dreamed of being in the battle and shooting down the gray-uniformed rebels. Unfortunately, by the time he was of age for conscription into the army, his mother had grown terminally ill. He had no choice but to stay and care for her. Nearly a year later, the old bird was still clucking and Jeremiah had not yet been able to enlist.

"Alright then," Father relented, "you go there and straight back. Understood, Winny?"

"Yes, sir." I promised, fingers crossed behind my back.

No sooner had the doors closed behind Jeremiah and I, that I began breaking my promise. "We only have a few minutes," I warned. "Even then, I'll most likely still get an earful upon our return."

"You and I both," Jeremiah concurred. "But, like the soldier said, the battle will soon be over and we will have missed our opportunity."

We ran in the opposite direction of the outhouse. "So, we have a decision to make. We can either climb the hill over yonder, or cross the stream and see if we can get a view from that copse of trees." Jeremiah pointed in the indicated direction.

I immediately responded with my choice. "The hill!" I nearly yelped the answer. Jeremiah shot me a quizzical look, and I sheepishly explained myself. "I have a fear of water," I answered, waving my hand towards the stream, which was really more of a small river. It looked to be nearly four feet deep in its center, and that was far too deep for more comfort.

We turned away from the stream and made our way up the nearby hill, taking care to stay low in the bushes. The minutes passed us by more rapidly than I had hoped for as we slowly climbed. With each moment of travel, my nerves grew more rattled. Not because the gunfire and smoke grew closer, but because every tick of the clock brought with it a harsher penalty from my father. I readily admit that I had misjudged the time it would take to climb the hill.

All nerves were quickly forgotten upon arriving at our destination, however. Once the hill had been crested, we easily saw what we had yearned for. Still a ways off, just enough for a bystander's comfort, we witnessed glorious battle. Two groups of men stood apart from one another. One group clad in gray, one in the Union blue – both interspersed with the mortal red of the battlefield. Each group had men falling, but noticeably the Confederates in gray seemed to be dropping in greater number.

Near the rear of the Confederate line, we could see men fleeing. Even in the few minutes we stared - mouths agape - we could tell the Grays were retreating in ever increasing numbers.

We had arrived just in the nick of time, it seemed.

The Union soldier had been correct. The northerners were winning the battle. Judging by the length of the skirmish, and the number of dead soldiers that could be seen littering the fields surrounding the town, I judged that this would be their first major victory of the war. There is no more awe-inspiring moment than to witness history being made firsthand, and being savvy enough to realize that fact while witnessing it.

"This is amazing," I whispered in elation. I assure you, whispering was wholly unnecessary atop that thunderous terrain, but our secrecy led me to speak lowly anyway.

I am sure that there had been a rustling of the bushes behind us, had we cared to hear it; but, if those warning sounds of stick and brush indeed existed, we failed to take notice. What was loud – too loud to miss even of a willful disposition – was the gunshot that rang out mere feet from where we crouched. While the loud report of the rifle stunned me, it was the sight of Jeremiah's head bursting - his warm blood heavily misting my face - which would be the first of many images that would henceforth forever haunt my dreams.

"Don't move!" a man donned in a gray uniform shouted as he burst forth from the bushes. "Keep your hands where I can see them!" A second man quickly joined him and, upon seeing me, both seemed as surprised as I was by the encounter.

CHAPLAIN

The second man slapped his compatriot on the shoulder. "Christ almighty, Singleton! He's just a boy." The man's gaze drifted to Jeremiah's lifeless body. "The one you shot's just a boy, too. Couldn't be more'n fifteen, by the looks of him."

The man standing with the smoking rifle in hand – Singleton, I figured – stared at the scene. His jaw hung loosely as he took it all in. I noticed his rifle aim dipping as the shock of the situation overtook him. I used the moment to try to slip off to the side. My movement thrust him back into reality, though, and he steadied the rifle's bore back onto me.

"I said don't move!" he shouted at me.

I stopped moving and kept my hands in the air.

"What we gonna do with him, Grimes?" Singleton asked his fellow soldier.

"Fuck if I know," Grimes shrugged. He considered it briefly and came to a conclusion. "I guess we can take him with us. A young lad may be about as handy as a Union boy if it comes down to it."

I didn't much care for where this was going.

"Yeah," Singleton agreed blankly, his eyes drifting away from me for a moment. After some thought, a smile creased his face and his eyes locked back onto me. "Yeah!" he repeated with more enthusiasm. "Good idea. C'mon boy, you're coming with us." Singleton motioned the point of his rifle towards the bush, indicating that I should start walking that direction.

Having no other choice, I obeyed.

******

We had walked for many hours, making sure to keep to the trees. The only stop that we had made was early in the journey. Singleton and Grimes had collected two rather large canvas packs from where they had hidden them in the trees. Rolled cloth tents we attached to the bottom of the packs. On Singleton's, I could also see the tip of a double-barreled shotgun protruding from between the rolled tent.

"Bet ya wished you had that damn thing during the battle," Grimes teased.

"Nah," Singleton replied. "Too damn easy to shoot one of your own with it."

We continued on until the sky had grown dim. We found a clearing in the trees and stopped for camp.

From the minute amount of conversation that had occurred on our march, I had surmised that the two men had been making their escape from the battlefield when they had stumbled upon me.

Cowards!

Perhaps I was judging a bit harshly, but I was in a fearful state. Not panicky, mind you – a certain excitement was undeniably mixed in, keeping the panic at bay – but fearful nonetheless.

It was the man named Singleton that engaged me in conversation first; his southern drawl heavily apparent.

"What's your name, boy?"

"Winfield. Though, you can call me Winny," I answered.

"Winny, huh?" He spit a wad of tobacco on the ground. "What in God's name was you doing up on that hill, Winny?"

"I wanted to see the battle," I admitted. "I just wanted a peek at it. I didn't think that I'd get much chance elsewhere."

"Why would you want to see somethin' like that? Men dying in the thousands! Blood soaking the ground. Much too gruesome and unfortunate to qualify as entertainment, wouldn't ya say?"

I shrugged. He had a valid point. I could feel a small amount of shame creeping into me as I considered his words.

"Anyway, I'm not about to apologize for taking you as our prisoner. Have no delusions on that. As far as I'm concerned, ya volunteered yourself by being foolish enough to leave whatever hole you had been hidden in."

Like a simpleton, I simply nodded.

CHAPLAIN

"Just so you know, my partner and I are taking you to meet up with some of our troop at an agreed upon spot near the base of the mountains. I don't expect to make it there for a couple more days yet," Singleton ejected another tobacco wad into the dirt. "The reason I'm telling you this is that we're going to be traveling hard and fast. We'll be pushing you to keep up. Ya hear?"

I nodded. Even as a child, I often found myself to possess few words in extreme situations.

"We have no plans of hurting you, but if you try to escape, we'll shoot you dead...sure as dog shit. We good?"

I nodded again.

With that, the conversation ended and we slept for the night.

July 5th, 1863

It ended up taking us two days to meet up with their troop. As promised, the pace had been rough, but not too intense that I couldn't manage.

Few words had been spoken directly to me, though I had been able to occupy myself by listening to the conversations between Singleton and Grimes. They told tale of the war thus far, which I found fascinating. And, also as promised, they treated me as well as could be expected.

With the mountains now starting to tower over our forward path, the first of their compatriots announced himself.

"Holy shit! Is that you, Singleton?" A gray-coated man rushed up to us as soon as we emerged from the bush.

"Yes indeed. We made it out just as everything started to go to shit."

The stranger walked up to Singleton and engulfed him in a large bear hug. "Us, too. As soon as General Lee started calling for a retreat, we hightailed it out of there." The man broke from the embrace and held Singleton at arm's length. "I'm glad you made it. You too, Grimes," he finished while shooting a glance in Grimes' direction. It was at that point that he noticed me for the first time.

"What's this?" he asked Singleton. "A boy?"

"Yep. We came across him as we was escaping. Figured he'd make as good a hostage as any in case we came across any Yanks."

"How old are you, boy?" the man asked.

"Nine years old, sir." I answered sheepishly.

"Nine years old, huh?" The man continued staring at me for a moment and then turned back to Singleton. "I don't think Captain Wilkes is gonna be too happy about this."

Singleton and Grimes glanced at each other, disturbed at the prospect of an upset Captain Wilkes.

"Well, Jenkins, we didn't have…" Singleton began but was quickly cut off by the man I now knew as Jenkins.

"Save it. I'm not the one you'll need to explain it too." The men stood in silence for a moment until Jenkins tilted his head back towards the larger group mulling around in the trees behind him. "C'mon," he huffed, "no sense in dawdling. Come report in."

We followed Jenkins to the rest of the men I had seen in the background. I counted seven more wearing the gray, bringing the total of this little troop to ten. As we approached, a weary looking man with an undeniable hardness in his gait, stepped away from the milling crowd to intercept us. As he neared, I noticed my three captors tense up and salute.

"Sir!" All three greeted with their hands to their cap brims.

The approaching man wore three horizontal stripes of a golden hue on each collar. I knew that this must be the aforementioned Captain Wilkes. Wilkes quickly returned the salute. "At ease," he ordered, followed by all four men dropping their hands. "Glad to see you boys made it." He smiled at his men, before turning to me. "And who might you be?"

"Winfield, sir, but most people call me Winny."

Before I could say anything more, Jenkins cut in. "He's a boy of nine, Captain. Privates Singleton and Grimes here came upon him as they were falling back from the battlefield and had no choice but to bring him along, sir."

Wilkes gave a short laugh that contained no trace of humor. "Had no choice but to kidnap a child, huh? What? Was he threatening you, Private Singleton?" Wilkes got into Singleton's face when he barked the question. Singleton appeared too frightened to answer, but he was saved by Wilkes' refusal to pause long enough for whatever feeble excuse was going to escape his lips. "That story should be a hoot when I get a chance to hear it."

"Sir," Jenkins cut in, "what would you like us to do with the boy?"

Wilkes considered me for a moment. He eventually dropped his shoulders and sighed. "Well, it seems to me that we have no choice but to keep him for now. We're setting up camp here for the night and I wouldn't want this boy to bring any Yanks back to intrude upon us during the night." Wilkes pointed to a tent that had been set up near the rear of their impromptu camp site. "Take him over to where Corporal Stevens is standing guard and throw him in with the Yank soldier we captured." Wilkes glowered at Singleton and Grimes as he concluded his instructions. "A *proper* prisoner that was captured within the code of decency and honor, I might add."

Singleton and Grimes shirked at the rebuke, but did as instructed, leading me over to the indicated tent. "And hurry back Privates! We need to go over the plan to rejoin General Lee back at the Potomac," Wilkes called after them as they marched me forward.

We arrived at the tent, the corporal eyeing me with suspicion. "Them Unis are getting younger every day, aren't they?" he asked Singleton while keeping his eyes on me. He followed this by spitting a large wad of tobacco juice on the ground by my feet.

"He's no Uni, Stevens. Just some boy Grimes and I came upon during the retreat."

"Well, why'd you bring him along then? This ain't no nursery."

Singleton shrugged. "It doesn't much matter anymore. He's here now and the captain says to lock him up with the Yank," Singleton explained.

The guard, Stevens, continued staring at me for a moment. After another obnoxiously large wad of spittle, he shrugged. "Well, if the captain says so." Stevens stepped out of the way of the tent's entrance to let us by. "Just make sure you tie him up real tight. If he's anything like the boys I grew up with, he'll be a wily one. Easy to escape if you don't cinch him up real good."

Singleton nodded at Stevens and led me into the tent. No sooner had we entered than I noticed the tent's only other occupant; dirt covering his blue uniform and his hands tied to a stake behind his back. The Union soldier looked up at us as we entered and looked as surprised as everyone else had been when he saw a boy my age being escorted in.

"Johnny Reb in the business of kidnapping little boys now?" the soldier asked, using the Union's derogatory term for the Confederate soldiers.

Singleton sighed. "I'm getting sick and tired of explaining this to every Tom, Dick, and Harry we come across. I'm sure as shit not going to be repeating myself to the likes of you, Yank," Singleton griped, roughly wrestling me to my rear. He grabbed some nearby rope and tied my hands to a wooden stake across the tent from the Union soldier. As Stevens had recommended, Singleton tied me damn tight.

With my wrists sufficiently hurting, Singleton stood and brushed his hands together, ridding himself of some sort of imaginary dust. "Well, you two just sit in here, all nice and cozy like, until one of us comes and gets ya." Singleton gave a short chuckle and exited the tent, leaving me alone with the similarly bound soldier.

At first, it was silent in that makeshift prison after Singleton departed. An oil lamp burned in the corner, keeping us in perpetual light. I assumed it was left burning to assist the guards in keeping an eye on us. I stared at the Union soldier and he stared back at me. He had an angry scowl on his face as he stared at me. I was deliberating with myself what it was that I could have possibly done to evoke this man's ire, when he finally spoke. "How badly did they hurt you?"

I realized then that he was staring at the crusty remains of Jeremiah's blood on my face and that his anger wasn't intended at me, but at what depravities the rebels may have inflicted *on* me.

"Oh, no," I corrected, "it's not my blood. They were quite pushy as they marched me along, but they caused no untoward harm towards me." His scowl loosened with my assurance. I went on to explain my capture and how I had been at fault for allowing my curiosity to get the better of me. His anger briefly flared at the telling of Jeremiah's fate, but had diminished some by the end of my tale.

"What's your name, boy?"

"Winfield, but you can call me Winny."

"Well, Winny, you can call me Silas. Full name's Silas Armington, 10th Regiment of the Rhode Island Infantry."

"Pleasure to meet you Silas," I nodded, as that was the limit of gentlemanly courtesy I could render, given that my hands were tied. "You're from Rhode Island?"

"Born and raised," Silas confirmed.

"I've never been there," I related.

"When we get out of here, we may have to remedy that," Silas encouraged with a promising smile.

"You think we'll get out of here?"

Silas didn't hesitate. "Of course. I may wind up in a prisoner camp for a while, but you'll be let go much sooner, I'd wager. General Lee, for all his faults, is not a monster. I knew him when he was the superintendent at West Point many years ago. I doubt he'll look too highly on these men imprisoning a boy of your age."

We chatted about many a-thing over the next while. The splendors of Silas' home state. My own home in New York. The horror my father was undoubtedly experiencing at my failure to return to the barn. The more I conversed with Silas, the more I grew to like him. He had a pleasant manner about him, and he seemed well versed in the tricky business of keeping nerves soothed and hopes alive. I never could coax from him much detail on his prior experiences in that disastrous affair of the early Sixties, but I fostered the notion that he had endured a great many hardships during his time in service to his country.

Soon we were brought a small serving of slop that I couldn't identify. Our bounds were released so that we could consume the wretched meal, though we were carefully guarded at gunpoint as we dined. The man who brought us our meal, a portly man who I later found was the camp's mess steward named Heber McCarthy, delivered our platters and exited the tent with one of his own. At least I knew that this abysmal fare was shared by all, and not just an extra punishment reserved for us captives.

McCarthy soon returned to collect our bowls and instructed us that we should do our best to catch some sleep. He preemptively apologized for our rough sleeping conditions, but made no further gesture to lighten our burden. He stopped at the oil lamp and removed a canteen from a satchel that he had carried in with him. He poured a small amount of liquid into the lamp's reservoir and then slid the canteen back into the bag.

"Kerosene," McCarthy explained, catching my curious glare. "Captain Wilkes somehow managed to procure some before we left. We use it for the lamps as well as to help get the campfires started. Works much better than the whale oil the army still mostly uses."

With that, he apologized again for the rough sleeping arrangements and departed and we were left in silence again.

Despite our uncomfortable postures, we both managed to drift off into the realm of unfettered dreams.

July 6th, 1863

I was awoken the next morning by a loud rustling of the tent's door; really just a flap of canvas that was secured at the bottom with a string. Our guard from the previous evening, Corporal Stevens, entered, looking agitated. He was accompanied by another rebel that I had not been introduced with, also appearing distressed. The second man bore the same two blue v-shaped chevrons of Corporal Stevens, so I knew him to be yet another corporal of the Confederate Infantry. They released the ropes tying our hands and marched us out of the tent at gunpoint.

Upon exiting the tent into the bright, but chilly, morning, I saw that the entire camp was awake, and seemingly in the midst of some sort of engagement; though the cause of the hurried activity I could not yet discern.

"Stevens! Holton!" Wilkes shouted to the men that had led us from the tent. "Set the prisoners here and keep your weapons trained on them."

Our two captors led us to the designated spot and roughly shoved down us to our knees. Once we were situated, they backed several paces away, but I could still feel the aim of their rifles digging into our spines.

"Sergeant Major!" Wilkes called out, eliciting a response from a grizzled man with a hard look in his eye. "Take control of the troops. Nobody fires until I give the go-ahead."

"Yes, sir!" the sergeant major snapped loudly. "You hear that, grunts?" he shouted out to the gathered force. As one, they sharply responded that they understood.

I was still trying to grasp the cause of the camp's sudden boisterousness, when a rustling came from the surrounding trees.

"This is Captain Henry Wilkes, of the Army of North Virginia! Be advised, I have guns trained on your position! Now, identify yourself before I give the order to fire!"

That is when I realized that Silas and I were being purposely being displayed as hostages, in the case that a Union presence had found Wilkes' camp.

The response from the trees was unexpected. "Thank the Lord Jesus!" A man poked out from the cover of the woods, adorned in the familiar gray uniform of his brothers-in-arms. "Southern boys!" he shouted.

"Indeed!" Wilkes shouted at the partially exposed man. "And who may you be?"

The man fully emerged from the covering, saluted, and then identified himself. "First Sergeant Thomas Colt, sir, of the 9th Regiment Alabama Infantry."

"What are you doing stalking around in my woods, Sergeant Colt?" Wilkes shouted.

"Sir, myself and the two others with me," Colt started to explain, pointing towards the trees behind him, "we are coming from the slaughter of Gettysburg. We pulled back under General Lee's order and are making our way into the mountains. We're planning to head south and circle around back to the Potomac."

"As are we, First Sergeant!" Wilkes informed. His tenor turned friendly, but I noticed that his posture remained stiff. "It looks like you may have stumbled into the right place. Have your men come out and join us." Wilkes offered the invitation, but I noticed that he had yet to order his men to lower their rifles. I knew then that Captain Wilkes was no slouch and was not the type to be easily taken off guard. If First

Sergeant Colt was attempting some sort of ruse, it most assuredly would not be well met.

"Yes, sir. Will do," Colt responded. "One thing, though, before I have them come out."

From the corner I my eye, I saw the sergeant major tense at Colt's delay. For some reason, the tension had just slipped back up a notch.

"What's that, First Sergeant?"

"We have with us a Yankee prisoner," Colt explained.

"Great! Another one…" I heard the sergeant major mumble.

"I'm sure we'd all prefer you not fire on us when you see a Union uniform emerging from our cover."

"Indeed, First Sergeant." Wilkes agreed. "Now bring them out so we can get on with our day."

"Yes, sir!" Colt responded, followed by a whistle towards the trees.

Another rustling erupted from the woods, followed by a man being roughly shoved out of some bushes. He stumbled forward and fell to his knees as two men in gray followed with their guns pointed towards his back. One of the men stopped and jerked the fallen man to his feet, pushing him forward towards the camp. He certainly wasn't gentle in doing so, either.

There were two things I initially noticed about this new prisoner. First, his uniform was mostly black, indicating that he was either a medical officer or in the chaplain corp. Second, his face. The entire right side was disfigured. It appeared as if his face, right of his nose, had melted at some point. Intense scarring distorted his features and his corresponding eye was without pupil. Just a white orb that floated amidst the scarring.

The grotesque-looking man was prodded unsteadily forward until he came crashing to his knees again, directly in front of Captain Wilkes. Wilkes eyed the man with suspicion, doing well to mask the disgust he must have felt, for the prisoner's face would have wrought revulsion in most men.

Wilkes pried his eyes from the scarred prisoner and seared his stare into Colt. "You are aware that untoward harm towards a medical officer is not authorized under the statutes of war, are you not?"

"I am aware, sir," Colt informed. "We have not unjustly harmed him in any way. Besides, sir, he's not a medical officer. He has identified himself as a chaplain."

"First a lad, now a chaplain?" the sergeant major griped. "Does no one around here know how to capture a proper soldier?"

If Wilkes heard the sergeant major's gripe, he chose to ignore it. Instead, he continued addressing First Sergeant Colt. "The same rules apply for chaplains, as I am sure that you are also aware. Either way, I hope that I do not learn of any unmerited abuse towards your captive here," Wilkes warned the stiff first sergeant.

"You will not, sir," Colt assured.

Wilkes nodded and swung his attention over to the new arrivals. "And what are your names?" he asked.

The question was met with silence. The soldier that had previously jerked the chaplain off of the ground, now smacked his palm upside the back of his head. "You heard the Captain. Answer!"

"Actually, my question was directed at you, Private," Wilkes corrected.

The private took in the Captain's words and quickly popped to attention. "Olmstead, sir! Private Mickey Olmstead of Cahawba, Alabama, sir!"

"Well, Private," Wilkes continued, "I was going to comment on how you were treating your prisoner, but seeing as how you just struck him *after* my warnings to First Sergeant Colt, I think we will be having that conversation in privacy."

I watched as Olmstead nervously gulped, then answered, "Yes, sir!"

Wilkes nodded at the private and finally brought his gaze towards the prisoner. He studied him further before addressing him. "You say that you are a chaplain?"

The scar-faced man nodded towards the captain, piercing him with his one good eye. He looked remarkably calm for a prisoner of war. Even I had been more visibly distressed upon my arrival, though I had considered myself to be far more accepting of my circumstances than most.

"If that is so, then why do you not wear the cross on your shoulder board?"

"I am *not* a chaplain of the cross," the disfigured man informed coldly.

A chill crept into my bones at the man's revelation.

"Then what are you a chaplain of?" Wilkes asked, his eyebrow raised. The prisoner remained silent. Seeing how the chaplain refused to respond, Wilkes changed his inquiry. "What is your name, then?"

This, the chaplain answered. "Lyman. Lyman Abernathy. President Lincoln himself appointed me with the honorary rank of Major, so you may call me Major Abernathy if you prefer. Though, I must confess, military stature does not interest me in the slightest."

"Sir," a voice intruded from behind Wilkes. It was one of the Wilkes' men at camp that I had not come to know at that point.

Wilkes turned toward the man who had spoken up. "Yes, Sergeant Tuttle, what is it?"

"Sir, I recognize this man," Tuttle informed the captain.

"With a face like that, how could you not?" Singleton joked, earning the glare of Captain Wilkes. Singleton quickly snapped back to attention and resumed his silence.

"Go on, Sergeant Tuttle," Wilkes prompted, letting his ire-filled gaze linger on Singleton.

"I saw this man during the battle. He was sitting atop the battlefield, on horseback, at the right hand of General Meade."

"He was with Meade?" Wilkes asked, wondering why this chaplain had been stationed directly next to the general leading the forces at Gettysburg.

"Yes, sir," Tuttle confirmed. "Private Singleton may have spoken out of turn, but he's not incorrect. His disposition is hard to mistake, sir."

Wilkes looked back down at Lyman Abernathy, as if to reassure himself of Tuttle's statement. "I suppose that you are correct on that front, Sergeant."

Wilkes knelt down so that he would be eye-to-eye with the captive. "So, how about it, Major? Is what Sergeant Tuttle tells me true?"

"About the hideous nature of my appearance? Or my being at the right hand of General Meade?"

"I am not a man that likes to play games, Major Abernathy. Do not test me," Wilkes warned.

"Please, call me Lyman. I am not a fan of such formality."

Wilkes remained silent, but looked like he would strike out at Lyman at any moment. Lyman must have seen this too, and he continued.

"As far as Sergeant Tuttle's statements are concerned, I confess both to be true."

I silently hoped for this interrogation to be over. Every word from Lyman's mouth deepened the chill that I was feeling in my bones. Looking around, it seemed that I was not the only one feeling it, as several of the surrounding men looked to be shivering, despite the rapid warming of the summer morning.

Wilkes stood, but kept his gaze on Lyman. "So you were at the right hand of General Meade, and you related earlier having personally met that charlatan in the White House." Wilkes took a moment's assessment of the kneeling chaplain before continuing. "Just who in the hell are you, Major Abernathy?"

Lyman did not answer the question. He only offered a short laugh in its stead. If his words had been chilling my bones, his laughter made them feel like they would soon crack.

Realizing Lyman wasn't going to answer, Wilkes ordered he be detained in the prison tent, as well as having Silas and I returned there.

I confess feeling much trepidation at the thought of being locked up with the strange chaplain.

The three of us were marched into the tent and each secured to our separate stakes. It was a small victory, but I silently praised the rebels for securing the chaplain to the stake furthest from me.

"Hopefully we don't get many more prisoners in this camp. We only have one stake left before we have to start sharing," Silas joked, trying to distract from the uneasiness that our latest addition leached into the tent.

The chaplain did not acknowledge the jest. Instead, his good eye unwaveringly bore into me. When he did eventually speak, the biting chill crept back into my bones. "You have nothing to fear from me, boy. You possess a dark beauty inside you. I can smell it." The working side of his mouth curved into a smile, the other half remained stagnant. It was his eye that caught my attention, though. It shone only with darkness.

"My name is Winfield, sir, but you can call me Winny." It was the only response I trusted my voice to enunciate without breaking down.

"Name's mean nothing, boy. In fact, you will come to learn that everything means nothing."

And that was as far as I was willing to go with that conversation. I retreated within myself and hunkered as low as my rearward bound arms would allow.

"Johnny Reb had a point," Silas cut in. I knew he was trying to divert the eerie man's attention away from me. "I, as well, saw you riding by the side of General Meade. Why was a chaplain helping to lead the charge against the rebels? I never figured George Meade for the religious sort."

Silas' tactic worked in that it tore Lyman's eye from piercing my soul. He turned to face Silas, the half-smile disappearing from his lips. "What is it to you, speck? Did your army not win the battle?"

"We did - or at least we were damn close by the time of my capture - but that doesn't answer my question."

"God's intervention will *always* result in success for those willing to accept it," Lyman answered coldly.

"That may be true. Despite their faults, the rebels are as much God-fearing people as any of us."

The chaplain chuckled. "What do you know of God, speck? What do the cattle in the fields – be they from the north or south, or even east or west – know of God? You are all blind, feasting on your cud and feeling blessed in your ignorance."

I admit that Silas was handling the situation much better than I. I listened to the conversation, but refused to emerge the shell I had built for myself.

"I apologize for my lack of manners, Major" Silas responded, attempting to change the conversation's flow. "I haven't properly introduced myself. My name is Silas. Ordnance Sergeant Silas Armington of the 2nd Regiment Infantry." Before Lyman could repeat his stance on names, Silas continued. "I inform you of this so you will no longer have to refer to me as speck."

The half-smile returned to Lyman's mouth. In truth, I preferred when his lips were flat, void of emotional context.

"Knowledge of whatever meaningless title was given to you does not change the fact that you are a speck," Lyman countered. "We are all but specks in the eyes of God."

The silence that followed was palpable. Just as it felt that the tension in the air would fill the tent until bursting, Silas inexplicably smiled and let loose a bit of laughter.

"I bet your Sunday masses are a real hoot!" Silas quipped. The darkness in Lyman's eye was replaced with ire. He looked away from us and left his gaze to linger on the tent's exit. He said nothing further - even adopting a semblance of peacefulness - but the wrath I had seen before he turned filled me with an undiscerning dread. I was, however, relieved that his attentions were no longer trained on me.

After the exchange, the silence permeated thickly. I was shivering with a fear that I could not comprehend and I assumed Silas was afflicted with the same. I tried several techniques of thought to calm myself. First, I tried thinking of my family, but that accomplished only adding dread and shame to my anxiety. Oh, how my father must have been filled with sorrow when I had not returned. I quickly dismissed that tactic. I then tried reflecting on some of my hobbies and interests, but found the thought of those to be depressing, as I was not certain if I would ever be able to enjoy such things again.

Finally, I settled on dissecting my current situation. I started by listing off all the inhabitants of the camp in my mind. On one side were Silas and myself. Of our captors, I had counted thirteen.

Captain Wilkes, of course.

My two original captors, Privates Willard Singleton and Lennie Grimes.

Singleton's friend, Corporal Beau Jenkins.

Our prison guards, Corporals Brent Stevens and Jerry Holton.

The mess steward, Private Heber McCarthy.

Sergeant Joel Tuttle, who I later learned was the camp's acting medic.

Sergeant Major Hirum Zollenger.

Then there were the new arrivals who had brought Lyman into camp.

First Sergeant Thomas Colt.

Private Mickey Olmstead, who I had already pegged as a man reeking of repugnance.

And, lastly, a man I would for a short time come to know as Private Grady Dalton.

Thirteen Confederates in all. Not great odds for escape. Luckily, Captain Wilkes seemed a decent man and a good soldier, so the need for that kind of adventurism felt limited.

Lastly, the man who, despite the Union colors that he wore, I had a strong sense was not aligned with either side. The chaplain Major Lyman Abernathy. Amidst the plethora of Confederates, if there was any one soul in the camp who brought forth the desire to flee, it was him.

Listing the names in my head - trying to recall certain ones that I had only heard once, maybe twice - somehow eased my fretful state.

The bliss I had found was all shattered in an instant, however, as the tent flap shook. It was flung open, and Mickey Olmstead appeared, a mischievous smile plastered across his face. Corporal Holton momentarily leaned into view, addressing Olmstead. "I'll go grab some coffee off the fire. Don't rough them up, though. Captain will have my ass if they wind up injured on my watch." He walked away and Olmstead stepped fully inside the tent, quickly followed by his traveling companion, Grady Dalton.

Dalton shut the ten flap behind them as Olmstead made a show of surveying the tent's occupants. "Well, howdy fellas!" he proudly greeted. "Fancy meeting such highly esteemed acquaintances here." He followed with a snide laughter.

"What are you doing in here, Reb?" Silas asked, voice filled with contempt for the intruder. "I don't think your captain would much appreciate this little form of insubordination here."

"He's not my captain, Yank!" Olmstead quickly rebutted. "I watched as my captain was kilt on the battlefield. A Yankee bullet straight through his skull." Olmstead used his fingers to mimic a gun going off against his temple.

"I believe the word your looking for is *killed*, you Southern ape," Silas corrected.

The smile quickly evaporated from Olmstead's face. He curled his fist into a ball and I could tell that he was intending to strike. He was stopped by Dalton, who grabbed Olmstead's arm before he could swing. "We can't leave any marks, Olmstead. Like the Yank said, we're not supposed to even be in here!"

Olmstead stood his ground and stared wrathfully at Silas. I halfway expected he would proceed with the strike, despite Dalton's warning. His scorn eventually faded, however, and he slowly unclenched his fist, letting the smile creep back to his lips.

"Dalton here is right, you know. I don't need to hit you now. I'll see to it that you get to spend some time at Castle Thunder. We don't house many military prisoners there, but I'll get you in, all special like. You'll suffer plenty there at the hands of Captain Alexander." Olmstead grinned. "He's got quite the reputation, that Captain Alexander."

I could tell that Silas wanted to argue further, but he held himself in check and remained silent.

Satisfied, Olmstead turned towards Lyman. "Now, the reason I paid y'all a visit tonight." Olmstead reached into his blouse and pulled out a clear, unlabeled bottle. Through the translucent glass, I could see a black liquid sloshing inside. "What in the Virgin Mary's cunt is this?" Olmstead asked, holding the bottle out to Lyman. "Is it whiskey? I know how you godly types seem to be the biggest alcoholics among us."

Lyman, who had spent the entire exchange with his eyes glued to the dirt, lifted his head until his eye was aligned with the other man's gaze. "It is whatever you most desire," was his cryptic answer.

Olmstead laughed. "What I *most* desire is Cindy Lou Jessup's cunt wrapped around my dick – the sweetest little belle you'll ever meet, I promise ya – but, seeing as how that's unlikely to happen, whiskey will suffice." He popped the cork out of the bottle and gave it a long sniff. Olmstead's eyes rolled towards the tent's roof and his smile deepened. "Mmm mmm! I'll be damned! I was right...it *is* whiskey! Smells like the good shit, too!"

"Let me smell," Dalton more asked than demanded, holding out his hand for the bottle. Olmstead handed the bottle over. Dalton began bringing the bottle to his nose, but suddenly stopped and shot Olmstead a worrisome look. "Are you sure First Sergeant didn't see you take this off of him when we searched him?"

"What kind of dumbshit question is that!?" Olmstead scoffed. "If he had, do you think he would have let me keep it? You know First Sergeant Colt's a stickler for the rules."

Dalton appeared to consider Olmstead's statement for a moment, and then brought the bottle up to his nose and took a large whiff. His lips curled into a smile that matched Olmstead's. "Well, hot damn!" he elated. "You dummy, Olmstead. This here's rum, not whiskey," he announced. He held the bottle at arm's length and examined its contents through the glass. "I haven't had a good rum since before the war started."

"Get yer damn nose fixed," Olmstead angrily scolded, roughly snatching the bottle out of Dalton's hands. "That is whiskey if I ever damned smelt it."

Lyman remained silent, but held a malevolent grin on his lips throughout the entire exchange. I squirmed against my post, the chaplain's grin not sitting well with me.

Olmstead rushed the bottle to his lips and took a long pull from it. When finished, he brought the bottle back down and smacked his lips together. "Damn! That's whiskey alright...and some mighty fine whiskey, at that!"

"What?" Dalton asked, dumbfounded. "Gimme that bottle!" He swiped the bottle back from Olmstead and let the contents pour into his mouth. He sloshed it around, looking to be contemplative, and then finally swallowed. "I don't know what kind of horse's shit they sell you in Georgia, but in Mississippi, we call this here rum," he chided.

Olmstead looked annoyed and ready to respond, when Silas spoke up again. "I was hoping it'd end up being poison," he muttered.

Olmstead quickly turned his attention from Dalton and rushed towards Silas. He didn't punch him, as he had nearly done previously, but he did poke him forcefully in the chest." Shut yer mouth, Yankee! If I hear another word leave that fuckhole of yours, I'll cut off the good chaplain's cock and use it to make sure you won't be able to follow it up with another." Olmstead withdrew his hand from Silas' chest and let the smirk return to his lips. "And I'll have you know, I had to watch as that bible-spouting fucker took his pisses on the way out here. Let me tell you, he may consider himself God's messenger to man, but I *assure* you he's God's gift to *woman*."

With that, Olmstead started chuckling and withdrew from Silas. He placed the cork back into the bottle and stuffed it back into his blouse. "With that Yanks," and speaking to me for the first time, "and future Yank, Private Dalton and I will now take our leave to find some nice, cozy place for curling up with this lovely red eye." Red eye being a popular term during the war, meaning liquor.

Olmstead blew us a kiss and departed the tent. Jerry Holton had apparently returned at some point and greeted them as they exited.

"Did you get what you needed?" Holton asked.

"Sure did, Corporal," Olmstead confirmed. "And don't you worry none, the prisoners are none the worse for wear." Holton took one glance at us, winked, and then closed up the tent.

The malevolent grin stayed pasted on Lyman's face throughout the night, keeping me in chills.

The sun soon rose on another day, but it felt to me like a year had passed.

July 7th, 1863

"Wake up, you dirty Yanks!" the shout pierced the tent's walls immediately before the flap was thrown open. Corporal Brent Stevens filled in the space vacated by the canvas sheet. "We're moving out."

I slowly pried my eyes open. As I said, I hadn't been sleeping – just a little in-and-out there towards the end – and I couldn't remember ever having been so tired in my life. One glance towards the still awake – and still sneering – Lyman Abernathy chased away any fogginess that had seeped into my brain.

I swung a quick glance over to Silas, who was staring at what appeared to be a magnetic compass, though I couldn't tell for sure. Whatever it was, he slipped it back into his pocket when he caught me staring.

"They let you keep that?" I asked.

"Nope. I had it hidden away when they searched me," he answered.

I didn't get a chance to ask him what he meant before Stevens entered. Jerry Holton followed his fellow jailor inside. One-by-one, they untied our wrists from the posts and retied them together, so they were now secured in front of our bodies. I knew this was to make it easier for us to walk, hence not slowing down the day's planned procession.

"Sure hope you boys have strong legs about ya," Holton teased as he was retying Silas' wrists. "We've got ourselves one helluva upward climb today."

"Upward?" Silas asked. "Up into the mountains?"

"Yep," he answered. "Captain feels we should head up into the Appalachians and use them as cover. Too many damn Yankees around these parts recently."

"I thought you were trying to get to the Potomac to rejoin with General Lee? A bit out of the way, wouldn't you say?"

Holton shrugged. "It's what the Captain wants. Besides, marching straight to the Potomac from here would place Washington directly in our path. Not the best plan if your uniform is gray."

Silas nodded his understanding and let Holton lead him out front of the tent. Stevens had Lyman already situated out there, then came back in for me. I followed him outside where he placed me in line next to the others.

Stevens whistled towards Grimes, who came running over to us. "Grimes," Stevens said once Grimes was in earshot. "Watch these three while Corporal Holton and I get this tent packed up."

"Roger, Corporal. I've got them."

Grimes proceeded to stand with us, his rifle slung across his back. Not in such a posture to make us unduly uncomfortable, but enough to keep us from trying to run.

After a moment of silence, Grimes caught my attention. "How you holding up, kid?"

I stared at him for a moment before answering. Not out of hostility or hatred; more of a curious stare. "Well enough, given the circumstances I suppose."

A brief flicker of shame crossed his features before he continued. "Sorry about dragging you along with us. I'd wager Singleton feels the same. We were just scared at the time. If we could do it over again, I, for one, would just let you be."

"And let my friend live as well, I suppose?" I wasn't going to let him off *that* easy. I had a pleasant moment then, as I witnessed his shame deepen.

"Yeah, I suppose for that too." He was looking down now, mindlessly kicking at some dead leaves. "Though, to be fair, we didn't know you was boys then. We didn't know that until afterwards."

I didn't allow him a "fair enough" or make any indication that I accepted his apology. I remained silent and let him stew in his dismay. Looking back, perhaps I should have. Singleton and Grimes had seemed to be decent enough men and had treated me fairly on our journey to meet up with the rest of the troop.

Honestly, I was just thanking the heavens that it hadn't been Mickey Olmstead that had captured me.

Speaking of Olmstead, an intense coughing came from our right and I turned to see him exiting his tent, soaked in sweat and looking quite ill.

"About damn time, Olmstead," Singleton jested, approaching Olmstead. "Captain wants us ready to go in fifteen." Singleton then noticed Olmstead's sickly disposition as I had. "Jesus, Olmstead, you look like shit."

"Fuck you, Singleton!" Olmstead responded. "Your face looks like a whore's cunt scab," he remarked between coughs.

Singleton laughed at the insult. "Well, hon, you keep talking dirty like that and I'll have to give you a nice, long kiss with this cunt scab."

Singleton continued laughing as he walked over to the roaring campfire to pour himself some freshly heated coffee. Olmstead rolled his eyes and turned back towards his tent, muttering under his breath. "Fucking nancy."

I surveyed the campsite and was surprised to see how efficiently everything had been torn down. It was a stark difference from what I had grown accustomed to. Other than Olmstead's, which was already well on its way to being packed away, I only noticed one remaining tent standing. I was still wondering why that one had been left standing, when Sergeant Major Zollenger apparently noticed it as well.

"What the fuck is this shit!?" Zollenger roared as he swiftly trod towards the remaining tent. "Dalton! Wake your ass up!"

Olmstead briefly glanced over at the scene, an expression of concern crossing his pallid features.

Zollenger arrived at the tent and began banging on its side. "Get your ass out here now!" he commanded. "Don't think we won't leave you behind. Give the Yanks something to have fun with."

A loud coughing erupted from inside the tent, followed by the flap opening and Dalton spilling out of it. His appearance was at least as horrible as Olmstead's. More so, really.

Zollenger took a step back at seeing the sickly body that had fallen from the tent. "What the fuck's wrong with you, boy!? You catch the plague?"

Dalton coughed, but shook his head. "No, Sergeant Major. Just feeling a bit ill is all."

"What is it?" Zollenger continued prodding. "Can't handle this nice, country air?" Zollenger waved his hand around to indicate the surrounding countryside. "Or is it just that your pansy ass body is unable to handle all of this physical activity?"

Dalton continued coughing, unable to answer. He continued shaking his head, though.

"Sissy boys like you should have joined the Navy!" he spat. "You've got ten minutes to get packed up or we're leaving your ass behind. If you haven't fallen over dead by then, that is."

"Yes, Sergeant Major," Dalton managed to squeak out as Zollenger turned and stormed off towards the fire, the promise of its mud-colored brew surely on his mind.

I chanced a look over towards Lyman. He looked unmoved from his countenance during the night, still holding the sneer on his face. If anything, the scene with the two sick men had served to deepen his sinister grin.

******

CHAPLAIN

"God in Heaven!" Corporal Stevens cursed. "I can't remember a time that my legs burned this badly."

I had to agree. Having still been only a lad, possessing the overabundance of energy granted to youth; even I was feeling the strain of the day's march. Captain Wilkes had chosen our path, doing his best to keep us in the lower mountain passes, but still, it seemed that we had been climbing most of the way.

Though the high peaks hid the exact position of the sun, the slight dimming of the sky led me to understand that night would soon be closing in. I estimated that we only had about an hour of sunlight remaining and I was looking forward to Captain Wilkes finding us a nice area to settle for the night.

I cringed as another coughing fit erupted behind me. Either Olmstead or Dalton, I wasn't sure. Their coughing had not subsided throughout the day. I hadn't a clue as to how they had kept up with the procession, but, despite us having to occasionally slow for them, they had somehow managed.

"Jesus Christ almighty," I heard Zollenger yelling behind me. "You two shit shingles are really starting to piss me off!"

I suppose the Sergeant Major's boots in their ass had played a major role in their making it this far.

I heard behind me a sound like a large sack of potatoes hitting the ground, then the Sergeant Major yelling "Halt!" The troop stopped the march, the sound of men dropping their bags on the ground and sighing with relief broke out down the line. Captain Wilkes appeared from near the front of the troop and hurriedly strode back towards Zollenger.

"What's the hold up, Sergeant Major?" Wilkes asked, annoyance more than concern in his tone.

I turned to see Zollenger standing over Dalton, who had collapsed onto the ground. He now looked significantly worse than Olmstead, though Olmstead was still quite a mess.

"I think Private Dalton here is on his last leg," Zollenger informed the Captain before leaning down and screaming in Dalton's ear. "Get your ass up, soldier!" He followed this by a rough kick in Dalton's side. Dalton hardly seemed to notice the abuse.

"At ease, Sergeant Major," Wilkes ordered calmly.

Wilkes leaned down towards Dalton, though he was careful to keep his distance from the ailing man. "Can you continue on, soldier?"

Dalton lifted his head to look up into Wilkes' eyes. He erupted into another coughing fit, but eventually nodded and started to pick himself up. He was nearly to his feet when his knees wobbled and he collapsed back into a kneeling position. His waist curled and he let loose a geyser of vomit onto the foliage.

Wilkes took a step back from Dalton at witnessing the man's regurgitation. Though I was several feet away, I subconsciously retracted a few steps as well.

The puddle Dalton had expelled was a foul mixture of black and red. More explicitly, it shone crimson with chunks of congealed black floating in it.

"Jesus!" Wilkes exploded at the sight. "Sergeant Major!"

Zollenger shot to attention. "Yes, sir?"

"We're going to be stopping for the evening soon. See to it that this man is quarantined once camp is set up."

"Yes, sir!"

Wilkes considered Olmstead for a brief moment. "This one too," he instructed.

"Roger, sir." Zollenger acknowledged. "I'll see to it personally."

"Good," Wilkes nodded, turning back towards the front of the procession.

"Captain?" Dalton moaned, stopping Wilkes in his tracks. He turned his attention back to the ashen man.

"Yes, Private?"

"Sir, please don't quarantine us. We ain't sick..."

"Shut the fuck up, Dalton," Olmstead warned.

"Sergeant Major," Wilkes said, looking annoyed by Olmstead's intrusion.

"Yes, sir?"

"If Private Olmstead speaks another word, shoot him in the head."

A shocked look briefly crossed Zollenger's face, but he quickly recovered and withdrew his pistol, placing it against Olmstead's temple. "Yes, sir."

Olmstead was stunned as well, but wisely kept his silence.

"Now," Wilkes continued, addressing Dalton, "why would you say that you're not sick? Do you not see that putridness that you just heaved up."

"I see it, sir," Dalton humbly acknowledged, "but we're not sick! We were poisoned."

I could hear murmurs break out behind me. Dalton's announcement obviously coming as a surprise.

"How so?" Wilkes asked.

"The chaplain, sir. He poisoned Private Olmstead and me."

The rustling behind me increased. A glance to where Lyman was standing revealed Stevens' rifle inching up towards the man, Stevens having just grown more suspicious of the chaplain. Also, I should note, Jerry Holton, who had let the men in the tent the previous evening, started growing nervous as well.

Wilkes looked skeptical of Dalton's accusation. "How, may I ask, did a bound prisoner manage to poison two of my soldiers?"

The rustling behind me grew silent as the men grew still, waiting for Dalton's answer.

Olmstead looked ready to utter another threat to Dalton, but held his tongue as Zollenger's pistol dug a little deeper into his flesh.

"Well, sir," Dalton began, "Private Olmstead found a bottle on the chaplain when we first captured him. We figured it was some kind of liquor so he hid it away until we had a chance to imbibe on it. Which we did, sir. Last night." Another cough, this one wet and wheezy. Then: "It ended up being some kind of rum, but I'm not sure what else the chaplain put in it."

Wilkes stood silent while processing Dalton's confession.

"I'm sorry, sir. I know that what Olmstead and I did was wrong," Dalton continued.

"That you were, Private," Wilkes rebuked. "I could have you men shot for disobeying direct orders."

"Yes, sir," Dalton replied before breaking into another fit of coughing.

Wilkes threw a disgusted look at Dalton and stepped away towards Olmstead. "And where is this bottle now, Private?"

Olmstead looked like he was about to deny Dalton's story, but he relented and extracted the bottle from its hiding place. I noticed that there was still a small amount of the black liquid resting on the bottom. Olmstead extended the bottle out to Wilkes. "Here, sir. And it's whiskey, not rum."

"Does the Captain look like he gives two fucks which spirit is in that bottle, Private!?" Zollenger reprimanded, applying more pressure to Olmstead's temple.

"Thank you, Sergeant Major," Wilkes nodded towards Zollenger, before turning back to Olmstead. "Indeed, I do not." He took the bottle from Olmstead and popped the cork out of it. "However, if there is poison in here, I most definitely do care." Wilkes held the mouth of the bottle to his nose and breathed in the scent. A curious look crossed his face and he stared up into Olmstead's eyes.

"Are you two a couple of damn buffoons?"

Olmstead startled, unsure what Wilkes was getting at.

"I don't know where you two were raised, but I hate to inform you that this is neither whiskey nor rum," Wilkes informed. "You two idiots were sneaking around with a bottle of Georgia tea."

Confusion emanated brightly from both of the sick men's faces.

"I wouldn't shoot a man for having some tea on him," Wilkes mocked. "Though, maybe for hoarding it to himself, I suppose I might."

I was a bit thrown by hearing a jest emerge from the captain's mouth. Apparently the man had a sense of humor after all.

"Strangest damn tea I have ever seen," Zollenger remarked, not sharing in the humor. He was eyeing the black liquid at the bottom of the bottle.

Wilkes studies the liquid, as if he hadn't noticed it at first. "Yes. Strange indeed. Perhaps the tea has spoiled somehow, though I have never heard of such a thing."

"Could it be that these two jackasses got themselves some type of food poisoning, then?" Zollenger asked.

Wilkes considered it. "Possibly. If so, it may well have been unintentional on the chaplain's part." Wilkes shot a suspicious glance at Lyman.

"Either way, to be safe, my original orders stand. Quarantine these men once camp has been set," Wilkes commanded. Olmstead and Dalton both turned their eyes downward at the announcement, possibly looking even more ill than they had before.

Wilkes tipped the bottle over, letting the black liquid spill out into a pool on the ground. Lobbing the bottle into the trees, he walked back to his place in front of the column. "Break's over, men! I want to get another half hour in before we set up camp. Let's move!"

Affirmations broke out down the line and the men prepared to resume their march into the mountains.

Before I turned away, I caught one last look at the pool of black liquid that Wilkes had poured from the bottle. It was just lying there, stagnant; as any puddle of liquid should. However, I couldn't shake this eerie feeling I got when looking at it.

It looked - for lack of a better word – *evil*!

* * * * * *

True to his word, Wilkes stopped the march half an hour later. If I had had a clock on me, I would have wagered that it was exactly thirty minutes on the dot.

The men flung their heavy bags to the ground with raucous sighs all around. After a brief moment's rest, Zollenger stomped over to

McCarthy and grabbed the kerosene canteen from him. "Jesus, McCarthy, this canteen is almost half empty now. You've been using too damn much of it. This shit's got to last us until at least Richmond."

"Yes, Sergeant Major," McCarthy replied.

Zollenger grabbed a couple sticks and splashed a very minute amount of the fuel onto them. He pulled a flint and some steel from his pocket, then struck them together over the sticks. It took a couple tries, but eventually the sparks they produced caught on the kerosene and the sticks began glowing with orange flame.

"Singleton!" Zollenger barked. Singleton ran up to him. Zollenger handed Singleton the canteen and informed him that he would be carrying it now. Also, that he would be using it as sparingly as possible.

With the fire now burning, and a pot of coffee warming in its flames, the men went about rebuilding the camp. The tents rose in an impressively organized fashion. Including the prison tent, which we had then been expeditiously secured inside.

Having lit the oil lamp to keep us in flickering light, Corporal Stevens exited the tent to assume his guard duties, leaving the three of us alone once again.

Almost instantly, I began nodding off. The previous night's lack of sleep, and the extreme nature of the day's exertions, had taken their toll. I was sure I would have no issues with sleep this evening.

And sleep I did. Out like a baby. Until, at one point deep in the evening, I was awoken. It was a rustling at the tent flap that had brought me out of my slumber. My sleep had been deep, and the rustling of the canvas not loud at all. I am unsure of how I came to be pulled from my world of dreams, but somehow I was.

At first, I was unsure of what my newly opened eyes were seeing. A black worm was squirming its way through the bottom fold of the flap. Once fully inside, it rose up on its hindquarters and seemed to survey the room, stopping to look at each of the occupants in turn, despite not appearing to have any eyes. It wasn't large; bigger than a garden variety earthworm, but smaller than a typical snake. Perhaps half a foot in length and two inches in diameter. Its most remarkable feature being the absolute blackness that it exuded, almost as if the light from the lamp was sucked into a void as it made contact with the thing's oily flesh.

I knew instantly what it was that I beheld; but, in this case, knowledge provided no comfort.

My mind rebelled against the notion, but my heart knew the worm to be the contents of the spilled bottle from earlier. Somehow, it had rose from a stagnant puddle and formed as this worm, having followed us from where we had abandoned it in the dirt.

An intense fear rushed through my body, much worse than anything I had felt to that point. I glanced back towards Silas, but found that he had not been awakened as I had.

"Boy!" I heard from where Lyman sat tied to his post. I reluctantly looked over at him and found him staring in my direction. My voice was locked in my throat, so I was unable to offer him any acknowledgment. Seeing he had my attention, he continued anyway. "Watch, boy. Watch and see God's hand at work."

Saliva filled my mouth, but I was unable to swallow it down. I sat and watched as the black worm wriggled its way to the Chaplain. I briefly thanked God - though that deistical title had already started to sour in my mind - that the worm was not crawling towards *me*.

The worm reached the chaplain's leg and then slithered its way up onto it. Unhindered by the near vertical rise as it reached Lyman's waist, it slinked further up until it was perched directly in front of his lips.

"Jesus took bread, broke it and gave it his disciples, saying 'this represents my body'," Lyman recited to me with his lips twisted into an eerie smirk. I recognized the words from church as those of Christ at the Last Supper, however there was nothing holy about them coming from the mouth of *this* chaplain.

"I'm sure you realize that the false Jesus has nothing to do with what is going on here, but the idea of the sacrament is compelling, is it not?" Lyman continued.

I still had no way of forming words, so I did not answer; though I have no clue at all to what I would have said had I been able to.

Lyman turned from me to lovingly smile at the black worm. I had a feeling that he would have gladly pet it if his hands had not been bound. "This bread before me is not just a representation, but an *actual* piece of the body of the true God. I partake of it, in remembrance and obedience to him."

Lyman once more turned his wicked grin upon me, and imparted to me one last word.

"Amen."

With that, the worm curled back and struck like a snake, shooting itself into Lyman's mouth. Black slime from the worm's body clumped on his lips as the worm forced its way through. I could see Lyman's throat expanding as the worm made its way down the tight passage, its cylindrical body clearly defined through the man's ashen skin. My eyes were stuck in horror until the worm had completed its passage and Lyman's throat resumed its normal architecture.

The grotesque scene seemingly concluded, the chaplain laid back against his pole, glowing with an almost postcoital satisfaction. At the very least, though, his attentions were no longer on me.

I had the urge to vomit, but I was too frozen in fear for my body to even manage that usually automatic task. I wasn't sure when, or even if, my body would ever let loose from the absolute terror that was gripping it. There was one thing I did know for sure, though...

I was about to suffer through another sleepless dawn.

July 8ᵗʰ, 1863

The sun's brightness seeped through the seams at the tent's door flap, announcing that morning had arrived. It wasn't long after when I could hear the camp come to life. The sounds of tent's rustling as men exited them, several yawns, and lumbering footsteps that carried still half-asleep bodies towards the crackling fire in promise of warmth and a hot mug of coffee.

Not much talking at first; just some low mumbles of morning platitude. The dawn carried on that way for a short while before Sergeant Major Zollenger's sharp voice shattered the peaceful morning air.

"Alright, ya sleepy ninnies, stop your slacking and start your packing! Captain wants us moving in thirty!" A low grumble rolled through the camp in response. "I believe the correct response would be 'Yes, Sergeant Major!'" Zollenger answered the grumbles.

Several "Yes, Sergeant Major" calls rang out, though all of them lacking conviction.

Soon thereafter, Stevens and Holton came into the tent and led us out in much the same fashion as the previous morning. This morning, though, I took care to keep an extra step or two between myself and the still-grinning chaplain. I considered now, much as I had for most of my wakeful night, informing one of the soldiers of what had transpired with the black worm, but I had a feeling that any utterance of mine would be quickly disregarded and written off as the fanciness of a childhood imagination.

Our two guards once again placed us under the watchful eye of Grimes as they retreated to pack up the prison tent, and I was left watching as the camp was dismantled. I looked over to where Jenkins was standing near two tents that had been set up away from the others. He had drawn guard duty for the two quarantined soldiers. Zollenger plodded towards him and Jenkins snapped to attention as he saw the Sergeant Major approaching.

"Jenkins!" Zollenger called out as he neared Jenkins.

"Yes, Sergeant Major?"

"How did our boys fare last night?" Zollenger asked, letting his tone soften with concern.

"Well, Sergeant Major, I have nothing significant to report with either one. Private Olmstead slept through the night with a heavy snore. Private Dalton mostly just moaned. He sounded quite restless, but he didn't try leaving or anything, so I let him be."

I noticed then that the low moaning sound Jenkins spoke of was still emanating from Dalton's tent. Hearing the anguish those moans held, coupled with my newfound knowledge of the black liquid, sent shivers shooting down my spine. I grew increasingly convinced that something horrible was happening inside that tent.

Zollenger considered the report for a moment and then strode over to Olmstead's tent and smacked his hand against the fabric. "Olmstead, you alive in there?"

The tent rattled as something inside moved towards the flap. I held my breath, unsure of what was about to emerge. After a long, uncomfortable moment, Olmstead popped his head out of the tent, turning it to stare up at Zollenger. Seeing it was just Olmstead, actually looking much better than the day prior, I took in a deep breath that I hadn't known I had been holding. I am unsure of what I had been expecting, but it most certainly wasn't that. He was still slightly pale, coupled with a minor sheen of sweat glistening from his forehead, but his appearance had significantly improved.

Zollenger noticed this, too.

"I must say, you're looking much better this morning, Private."

Olmstead nodded. "Yes, Sergeant Major. Feeling much better, too." Olmstead hacked up a chunk of phlegm onto the ground and then cleared his throat. There was no black, nor red, in the phlegm; just the normal sickly green.

"I'm glad to hear it," Zollenger said with legitimate relief in is voice. "Go ahead and get packed up then. We're moving out in thirty. I'll see to it that one of the men brings you over some breakfast and coffee."

Olmstead nodded and thanked the sergeant major, who was already swiftly advancing to Dalton's tent. He banged the fabric and yelled out, "Dalton, how about you? You alive in there?"

The only answer was the moaning sound, though it ratcheted up a bit.

Zollenger rattled the tent some more. "Wake up, shit bird!"

Still, only the moaning.

"Ah, hell," Zollenger muttered, stepping to the front of the tent. "You better be dying in there, Dalton!" he hollered as he flipped the flap upwards. From my vantage point, I couldn't see inside the tent, but I did see the inside of the flap as it came up. The canvas was splattered with the black goo.

Zollenger, however had a great view inside the tent, and what he saw morphed his stern scowl into a look of terror. He quickly released the tent flap, letting if fall back closed, and backed away several paces. "Sergeant Tuttle! Grab your medical bag and get your ass over here, ASAP!" he screamed out with a slight tremble in his voice.

Joel Tuttle expeditiously appeared, carrying a brown medic's bag with him. "Here, Sergeant Major," he announced on arrival.

"Tell me what in the blue hell is happening to Private Dalton," Zollenger ordered, pointing towards Dalton's tent.

Tuttle briefly stood still, radiating confusion. He first looked towards the tent, back at Zollenger, and seeing the impatient look on the sergeant major's face, quickly trotted to the tent. He set the medical bag down, threw open the tent flap, and peered inside. In only enough time for his mind to process what his eyes beheld, Tuttle recoiled.

"Fuck Dixie!" he blared as the flap fell shut. Tuttle held a muddled expression as he looked back over to Zollenger. "Sergeant Major, I'm only an *acting* medic. I gleaned a little medical knowledge off my pa, but never attended medical school or nothing. I know enough to patch up some wounds, even saw off a limb or two if need be, but I don't know much at all about diseases. We need a real doc for something like this."

"Well, do *something*, goddammit!" Zollenger commanded, appearing increasingly flustered. "We can't just leave the man like that and we don't got a real doc with us. Just you!"

Tuttle beseechingly looked around for something – *anything* – that could help up with his precarious situation. His eyes eventually settled on the medic bag near the tent. He rolled his eyes and huffed, before running over to it. He opened it up, rifled through the contents, and finally withdrew a leather apron from inside. Tuttle donned the apron, took two deep breaths to steel himself, then threw the tent open once more.

He was momentarily startled into inaction once again, but quickly caught himself and started reaching into the tent. He quickly thought better of it, and hurriedly withdrew his hands. He glanced around again, his eyes settling on his apron. He tucked his hands into the back of the apron and proceeded utilizing the leather as a type of mitt to grab hold of Dalton's boots. A piercing shriek of pain blasted from Dalton as Tuttle dragged him out onto the open forest floor.

A sharp gasp echoed throughout the camp at the sight of the man's body as Tuttle dragged him from the tent. Dalton had withered to roughly half his normal size. It was hard to distinguish exactly how emaciated he had become as his body was drenched in black ooze. He was almost completely covered in glossy black, only small patches of his ashen skin peeking through.

The moans had grown louder, now being accompanied by a loud sobbing interrupted only by intermittent shrieks. A shrill sucking sound could also be heard as Dalton tried desperately to draw in breath.

"Sergeant Major, report!" the blaring sound of Captain Wilkes' voice broke through the sickened camp. The man quickly followed, rushing towards the grisly scene.

Hiram twisted towards Wilkes, appearing to have a hard time forming his words. "Uh...uh...Captain..." he trailed off before gathering himself. "Sir, it's Private Dalton." He pointed towards the decrepit form sprawled out on the ground. He hadn't needed to, though, as Wilkes had already caught sight of him and was staring on in wide-eyed fascination.

"Jesus, Mary, and Joseph," the Captain sputtered, unwittingly making the sign of the cross over his body. "What the hell is wrong with him?"

Hiram shrugged; either unwilling, or unable, to say that he didn't have a fucking clue.

Wilkes' eyes, as well as everyone else's, grew even wider as the black ooze started to disappear from Dalton's bloated form. I strained to look closer as I could not believe what I was seeing. It appeared that the ooze was being sucked back into the man through his pores. As the ooze absorbed into his body, Dalton's thin frame began filling back in until he was near his normal size again.

But then it continued.

By the time his pale skin was completely exposed, looking as if he had just bathed all the muck off of him, Dalton had expanded to twice his normal size. He reminded me of a dead calf that I had found out in field once; bloated from a death that had occurred many days earlier.

It was then that Dalton began to speak. Only it was more of wheezy whisper than an actual voice emanating from his lips. I had to strain to make it out, but I'm pretty sure he was telling somebody to kill him.

Tuttle began reaching a hand towards Dalton. To do what, I am sure I will never know. He didn't get far though, as thick spouts of black shot out in unison; geysering from his every pore and splashing down to collect on his skin. He was completely covered now. No skin had been left exposed.

Tuttle had instantly snapped his hand back as soon as the black liquid had appeared. He instinctively retreated several feet away from the oily personage.

I could see through the muck that Dalton had shrunk back down to his previously atrophied shape. He let out a loud scream, filled with a kind of agony that would haunt my dreams forever. Then, louder now than before, he wailed, "Kill me! For the love of God, kill me!" A jet of black ooze then burst from his mouth, cutting off his further pleas.

Dalton said nothing more after that. He merely took in a huge gasping breath while his body once again retracted the black ooze in through his pores. This time his body, in its bloated form, stopped squirming and Dalton lay still.

I watched as an inky blackness flowed from the edges of his eyeballs until it had consumed them completely. His newly black eyes loosely rolled in his skull, and then the lids shut, closing them off from sight.

The silence that followed throughout the camp was palpable as every single person was staring at the dead, bloated body lying on the ground. The only sound I could hear at all was a bird chirping away merrily in the distance. Even the breeze had seemed to veer away from this cursed place.

It was Captain Wilkes that found his voice first. With his eyes still planted on Dalton's body, "Private Grimes?"

Grimes, whose gun was shakily pointed in our direction, responded, "Yes, Captain?"

"Please escort the chaplain over here and place him on his knees," Wilkes ordered, his tone flat and weary.

"Yes, sir." Grimes took a brief moment to compose himself and then dug the point of his rifle into Lyman's back, prompting the man to move forward. "You heard the captain. Move!" he instructed, marching the chaplain forward.

Lyman offered no resistance, walking forward and willingly collapsing to his knees in front of Wilkes.

Wilkes held his gaze on Dalton's still body for a moment longer, then slowly inched it over to the chaplain. Catching the entire camp off guard, he swiftly broke his sidearm free of its holster and jammed the barrel against Lyman's forehead. "What in the hell did you have in that bottle, Major?" he demanded.

Lyman's scarred face twisted into a hideous grin as he answered. "Simply an offering of the lord's own body. An offering that he has gratefully bestowed upon man."

Wilkes stared blankly at the chaplain. After a moment, he called out to Zollenger. "Sergeant Major?"

"Yes, sir."

"Have Sergeant Tuttle bring Private Dalton's body over here."

"Sir?" Zollenger asked, confused by the order.

"Just do it, Sergeant Major!" Wilkes snapped.

"Uh...yes sir!" Zollenger turned towards Tuttle. "Sergeant Tuttle!"

Tuttle gave no indication that he had heard the exchange. He was simply staring dumbfounded at Dalton's bloated form.

"Goddammit, Sergeant!" Zollenger screamed even louder. It had the desired effect as Tuttle startled loose from his trance and looked over to his superior. Seeing he had Tuttle's attention, Zollenger continued. "Did you hear the Captain's order?"

"No. Sorry, Sergeant Major."

Zollenger rolled his eyes. "Jesus Christ, boy! Get your balls about you and pay the fuck attention," he growled. Tuttle straightened up, once again looking soldiery.

"Drag Private Dalton's body over to the Captain," Zollenger repeated.

Tuttle considered the order for a moment, then, "With all due respect, Sergeant Major, I prefer not to get anywhere near that thing," he said, pointing at Dalton.

"Jesus Christ," Zollenger muttered, sympathizing with the sergeant's objection. He briefly thought it over before settling on a plan. "Alright. Here's what's going to happen. I agree you shouldn't be getting any of that black shit on you, so go and grab a couple blankets, wrap that damn body with them, and then drag his ass over here."

Sergeant Tuttle blinked a couple times, digesting what he had just been told. I could tell Zollenger was getting spun up for another bout of screaming, when Tuttle got ahold of himself and rushed off to procure some blankets, as ordered.

Zollenger watched Tuttle scramble off, then turned back to Wilkes. "If you don't mind my asking, sir, what are you intending to do with Private Dalton's body?"

"Well, Sergeant Major, since the good chaplain here seems unwilling to tell me what was in that little bottle of his, I'm going to make sure he gets a taste of his own medicine."

The captain's words had no apparent effect on Lyman, the chaplain's vile grin remaining steady as stone. I assume the Captain had been expecting to see fear ring in the man's eyes at his proclamation, but, if the lack of response bothered Wilkes, the captain did an admirable job of not showing it. Of course, after witnessing what I had the night before, I had a pretty good idea why Lyman wouldn't be scared of whatever infested Dalton's body. I almost spoke up then, but for some reason I never realized, my tongue was held in check.

The rest of the camp remained silent as Tuttle collected the woolen blankets for use on the bloated corpse. Having gathered three, he rushed back towards Dalton's body.

My eyes followed Tuttle as he ran. His eyes were unfocused, betraying the overwhelming thoughts that must have been flowing through his mind. His nerves were obviously on edge, panic coursing through him. Looking back, it should have come with little surprise when his feet caught on a fallen branch, partially hidden by the tall grass. He tripped forward, directly atop Dalton's remains.

As he fell, Tuttle managed to extend his arms to soften the blow, forcing the blanket between him and the body. As soon as the blanket -

Tuttle's full weight behind it - struck the body, the flesh sack that was Dalton burst open like a rubber balloon. Black ooze surged outwards like a dam had broken loose. Luckily, most of it flushed away from Tuttle, soaking into the ground on the opposite side of the body. The blanket blocked most of the rest, but his pant cuffs still wound up being covered in the sticky blackness. Only a few black droplets struck his skin. Mostly on his face and arms.

Tuttle immediately let go of the blanket and scurried backwards from the loose flesh pile, desperate to get away. Having managed several feet of distance, he started rapidly spitting onto the ground.

"Jesus Christ! Jesus Christ!" he cursed repeatedly, then: "That shit got in my mouth!" I hadn't noticed any splash into his mouth, but, judging by the multiple black dots covering his face, it wasn't hard to accept. "Oh fuck! Oh fuck!" he continued.

Tuttle's eyes radiated with an intense fear that I had never before witnessed in a man. His continued swearing and spitting a clear sign that he had lost control.

He looked around at his compatriots for help, but every time his gaze fell on one, they would instinctively recede from him. Tears welled up in his eyes and he started pounding the ground in pure frustration. He pleadingly searched around again, eliciting the same response as before.

It was when his eyes lit upon Lyman that his intensive fear vanished to be replaced with an equal amount of rage. Tuttle sprang from his place on the ground and rushed the chaplain. He crashed into Lyman, knocking him away from the barrel of Wilkes' pistol and onto the ground.

Wilkes had made no move to stop the private, instead stepping back a few paces from the possibly infected man as he and the chaplain rolled underneath.

Tuttle grabbed Lyman by the collar and shook him harshly, screaming into his face. "What the fuck is that shit, you son of a bitch!?"

Lyman's smile did not so much as flicker. Tuttle shook him again, only harder. "I asked you what the fuck that black shit is! Answer me!" Tuttle asked again, increasingly hysterical.

Smile still strong, Lyman sniffed loudly at Tuttle. "My, my, my," the chaplain began, his tone as merry as a songbird. "Aren't you the lucky man!?"

Confusion shortly dimmed the wrath in Tuttle's eyes, but couldn't hold the rage at bay for long. "How is that, you fucking cocksucker!? How could I possibly be considered *lucky*!?"

"God has decided not to make you wait. Much quicker than most, he gladly accepts you into his service." The tone was one of joy, but the spine-tingling sensation the words gave off was of the exact opposite.

"What the fuck does that mean, you fucking psychopath!?" Tuttle screamed, his shaking of the chaplain growing more intense. "One last time! What was in that fucking…"

Tuttle's threats abruptly ended. Only the sound of choking escaped his lips as his eyes grew wide in horror.

Tuttle abruptly released the chaplain and began pawing at his throat. He fell to his knees and hunched over, elbows smacking loudly into the dirt. He was attempting to suck in a breath, but was failing miserably.

Suddenly, a spasm jerked him upright with enough force that I could hear his spine crack. The momentum of the spasm was great enough to toss him backwards, leaving him sprawled on the grassy field.

I watched as his chest expanded. At first, I thought that maybe he had finally drawn in a breath, but the notion was quickly dispelled when his chest did not shrink back down, but instead, the bulge moved upwards towards Tuttle's throat. Much like Lyman's the night before, Tuttle's throat swelled out as something squirmed through it; only upwards this time, and much larger. The skin stretched to such a degree that its elasticity wasn't enough to compensate for the displacement. Small cracks ripped open in his flesh from the overexertion, blood quickly seeping out and running down to the grass.

Still, the mass traveled upwards.

Tuttle's mouth jerked open, a wet thud escaping as the mass inside smacked hard against the roof of his mouth. The thud came again, this time with enough force that the corners of Tuttle's mouth ripped open. Again the thudding sounded and Tuttle's cheeks split further apart, the bloody gash expanding. Then, one last time, and Tuttle's entire skull from the mouth up, burst upward and swung back, the remaining flesh at the rear of his skull acting as a hinge. His upper skull hung loosely, upside down, at the rear of his neck.

In its former place, a slimy, black tentacle rose up out of Tuttle's throat. Reaching nearly three feet long and a foot wide, it began swinging frantically around, emitting a high-pitch shriek from some unidentified orifice on its cylindrical body.

The tentacle first swung towards Captain Wilkes, who threw himself backwards, barely avoiding its grasp. Grimes, frozen stiff from fear, was not so lucky. The tentacle grabbed hold of him, wrapping itself around his arm and tugged, dragging him close. Some kind of smoke escaped from where the tentacle contacted Grimes' flesh. Grimes howled in excruciating pain. At first, it seemed that the tentacle was growing tight around the limb, constricting it like a boa. Watching further, I started to see that the smoking arm seemed more to be liquefying in the tentacles grasp, disappearing as if being absorbed by the thing's glistening flesh. It kept sinking deeper into Grimes' arm as the displaced flesh thinned the limb, until the tentacle was hugging against white bone. The smoking continued, as did the tentacle's tightening grip.

Grimes flopped backwards as he was finally released from his captured appendage, his arm now completely gone. The tentacle rapidly whipped out and grabbed him again, this time around the throat. Grimes wailed horrifically for several short moments, ceasing only when the flesh sealing his airway had finally dissolved.

The tentacle let Grimes' crumpled remains drop and moved off, towards Sergeant Major Zollenger. Zollenger immediately scrambled backward, away from the approaching horror.

Almost as one, the camp broke from their collective stupor and sprang into action. Maybe not action, necessarily, but they definitely sprang. Men scrambled around, most going for their rifles. Singleton and McCarthy retreated to their tents, while Olmstead ran to the nearest tree. Whatever had propelled Olmstead into fleeing must have worn off, because he stopped, curling into a fetal position at the tree's base, tears staining his face.

Silas turned and ran over to Stevens, who was the only man yet to rush off. His eyes were manic as he stood with his rifle pointed away from any meaningful target.

"Untie me," Silas demanded, holding his bound hands out to Stevens.

Stevens shook his head. "I...I can't do that."

"Come on, Corporal! I can help. Untie me!"

Stevens kept shaking his head, disbelief overtaking him from everything he had witnessed that morning. "No...no...I can't do that! You're a prisoner."

Silas pushed at Stevens forcefully, backing him up several steps. "Untie me, dammit!"

Stevens hurriedly raised his rifle, focusing its aim directly at Silas' head. "Stop right there! D...Don't move!" Fear had apparently overtaken Stevens, causing him to retreat into something he knew well; guarding prisoners.

"Fuck!" Silas yelled, realizing Stevens wasn't going to be made to understand. He turned on his heels and watched as the tentacle monster veered off from the escaping Zollenger and locked onto Jenkins.

Jenkins, who had been one of the men to retrieve his rifle, fired several shots into the beast as it approached. He might as well have been throwing pebbles. The thing barely broke stride each time a round connected with it. It easily kept coming. Jenkins backed away and kept firing until his rifle finally clicked on empty. He fervently reached into his pockets to retrieve more rounds, but ended up tripping over somebody's knapsack strewn on the ground. He tumbled over the pack, his back slamming into the dirt. The monster seized the opportunity and shot forward, squeezing its bulky mass around Jenkins' head. It coiled tightly and hefted Jenkins' entire body into the air. Jenkins' feet swung wildly and his muffled screams rang loud. I watched helplessly as his scalp, and eventually his skull, melted into the creature's flesh. Once his head had completely dissolved, Jenkins' body fell back to the ground, sounding like a side of beef being dropped to the floor.

The creature moved on.

Next, it found First Sergeant Colt. It rushed towards Colt as he fired several rounds into its advancing frame. As with Jenkins, the rounds had little effect, but Colt was able to get out of the way before the monster could latch onto him. He quickly scurried away, putting as much distance between the creature and himself as possible.

The creature stopped its pursuit in favor of a more opportune morsel of flesh. Its attention turned towards Jerry Holton, who repeated the actions, and the successes, of Colt. By this point, the monster had been turned back around in the camp and was left "staring" directly at Silas and Stevens.

Silas immediately turned back to Stevens. "Corporal, that fucking thing is heading this way, untie me now!"

"St...stay still or I'll sh...shoot!" Stevens stammered.

Silas turned his eyes back to the approaching beast and cursed. He turned to flee into the woods, but two shots from Stevens into the dirt in front of him stopped him cold. "Are you fucking kidding me!?" Silas yelled.

"Don't move or I'll...I'll..."

Silas ignored the rest and turned to see the creature had already arrived upon him. He knew that it was too late and collapsed into a ball on the ground, futilely placing his bound hands between the monster and himself.

Surprisingly, the creature moved right past him and continued towards Stevens. Stevens, his eyes filled with tears, finally let his attention be drawn to the fast-approaching nightmare and swung his gun up to meet it.

Far too late!

The creature quickly whipped out and snagged him around the head, same as it had done to Jenkins. A little higher perhaps, as Stevens' shrill bellows of pain weren't muffled in any way.

As Stevens' head was started steaming and disintegrating, Silas looked up from his crouched ball, surprised to still be alive. From his rear vantage point, he was looking straight at the flapping half-skull of Joel Tuttle. Silas' mouth dropped wide in shock.

I followed Silas's gaze to see what had him so fascinated. My sight now plastered on Tuttle's loose-hanging cranium, I was drawn to his eyes. They were glistening, full of tears which brimmed over their sockets, streaming down his forehead. They blinked and nervously fluttered about.

"Fucking hell," Silas moaned. "Tuttle's still alive!"

I knew Silas was correct. It seemed that the creature was keeping Tuttle alive somehow. Judging by the immense agony those eyes radiated, I too somehow knew, without a doubt, that Tuttle was fully conscious of all the immeasurable pain and horror of the abuse on his body.

I didn't know if that was the intent of the creature, but it sure seemed like a good bet.

Just as the final bit of Stevens' skull was being consumed, a loud boom shook the air and a large chunk of the monster's flesh evaporated. The divot in its flesh instantly filled in with the black sludge and reformed itself, but the shot had certainly been enough to draw its attention. I turned to see Singleton, now wielding the double-barrel shotgun I had first noticed during our initial escape from Gettysburg.

"You motherfucker! You killed Grimes!" he shouted putting another blast into the creature. It stumbled back far more than it had with the regular bullets, but wasn't deterred for long. Once again, the large chunk removed from its hide quickly healing.

"And Jenkins!" Singleton shouted again, blasting another round into the tentacle. "Should I keep going!?" he yelled, smoothly cracking the shotgun open and replacing the shells in both barrels. The monster used the time to recover and stumble further forward.

"This one's for Dalton!" he shouted, one-arm slamming the shotgun closed. "And I didn't even know that motherfucker!" He fired again.

"I think Singleton's lost it," I expressed to Silas.

He shrugged, but kept watching. I think he may have still been in shock from the revelation of Tuttle's consciousness. Or perhaps he was trying to figure out why he was passed up by the creature. I'm not sure which.

Singleton sidestepped the campfire as he slowly backed away, keeping his distance from the beast. He plugged another round into the tentacle's thick hide. "Corporal Brent Stevens!" he shouted with that blast.

Singleton reopened the shotgun's chamber and ejected the two spent shells. He jammed his hand into his pocket and quickly withdrew two more, but this time the creature didn't slowly lumber towards him. It took the full opportunity provided and charged. The tentacle whipped out to grab Singleton, but he realized what was happening quick enough to pounce backward, getting his body just out of the tentacle's range. Unfortunately, he had delayed just enough that the tentacle's tip managed to get a hold on the tip of his boot. It quickly seized the boot with its immense strength and yanked Singleton off his feet. A loud thud sounded from where his back crashed onto the hard ground.

Despite the hard landing, Singleton reacted quickly. No sooner had he impacted, that Singleton rolled off to his side. He managed to twist the tentacle enough that its black, glistening body came in direct contact with the campfire.

The tentacle emitted an ear-piercing squeal and immediately withdrew its grasp on Singleton's boot. The area that had touched the fire burst into flame with a loud whooshing sound. The fire immediately started spreading along its body, forcing the tentacle to slam itself down hard into the dirt. It rolled in the soil until the recently ignited flame was fully smothered.

Silas didn't miss a beat. No sooner had the flame gone out, he was charging towards the foul beast. "Oh no you don't," Silas murmured as he charged. The creature had unsteadily brought itself back up to Tuttle's feet, just as Silas lowered his shoulder and collided with the creature at Tuttle's broken spine. The Tuttle-monster tumbled forward, landing directly on the campfire. The tentacle's slime acting as if it were kerosene, the flame immediately sparked to life and engulfed the entire length of the black tentacle. The creature brought thrust itself out of the flames, wildly flailing through the air as it cracked and sizzled under the conflagration that had consumed it. Silas scrambled away from the frenzied creature, putting a safe distance between him and the swinging cylindrical torch. A deafening, ungodly shrieking pierced the air until the creature finally collapsed to its knees, then flopped forward onto the ground. It twitched a couple more times, then lay still.

The cacophony of activity ceased once the monster was dead; a hushed peacefulness left permeating the mountain air. I could hear weeping coming from Olmstead's curled body, but most else was quiet. Wilkes slowly marched forward towards the halcyon remains of the creature, which still shone with an orange flame. Occasionally, a pop would explode from the tentacle's consumed flesh and a few sparks would shoot out into the air.

Wilkes reached the beast and kicked at it, ensuring it was truly dead. Satisfied by its inertness, he ran his hand through his hair and surveyed the remains of the camp. His eyes briefly lingered on Olmstead's whimpering form, a look of disgust crossing his face.

Eventually, his gaze landed on Silas.

"Thank you for that, Sergeant."

Silas nodded. "Of course, Captain. I somehow doubt that thing much cared what color uniforms we wear."

"Indeed," Wilkes agreed, looking around the camp before turning back to the blue-clad sergeant. "I seem to be down a few men. Given these new horrors, wouldn't you agree that the more men the better if we want to escape these mountains?"

Silas hesitantly agreed, wanting to see where this was going.

"Good,' Wilkes continued. "I am inclined to free you from your bonds, but I ask that you stay with us until we reach Richmond. Once there, you have my word that you will be given safe passage back to Washington. Both you and the boy."

Silas let his eyes wander around the camp. Most of the men were still stunned, slowly recovering from the unexpected horror of the morning. A few of them were watching the exchange, though, interested in how this would play out.

"Are you going to untie us?" Silas asked. "We can be of greater assistance if another surprise awaits us."

"Corporal Holton!" Wilkes called out in answer.

Holton ran up to his Captain and saluted while answering. "Yes, sir!"

"Unbind Sergeant Armington and the boy. We'll no longer be needing to hold them prisoner." Wilkes shifted his attention back to us. "I think we've got bigger problems now than the Union army. Wouldn't you agree, Sergeant?"

Silas nodded.

Holton looked a little unsure of the order, but bounded over to us and untied our hands. No sooner had the rope fallen from his wrists, Silas ran over to the curled form of Olmstead and swiftly kicked him in his crumpled midsection. "You son of a bitch!" Silas screamed at the crying man. "This is your fucking fault!" He kicked him again.

Holton instinctively raised his rifle towards Silas, but Wilkes cut him off, motioning for him to lower the weapon. He did call out to Silas, however. "That's enough, Sergeant!"

Silas looked toward Wilkes. "He drank from the fucking bottle and started this whole damn thing!" Silas' own words prompted him to adopt a quizzical look. "Speaking of which, why the fuck is this asshole not a puddle of goo right now? Or even one of those fucking tentacle things?"

"God works in mysterious ways," Lyman casually answered from where he was still knelt. I realized that he hadn't moved at all during the attack.

At the sound of his voice, all eyes swung towards the chaplain. He resumed his silence.

"Yeah! Yeah!" Olmstead cried out, drawing Silas' attention back to the whimpering man. "He's the one to blame. The fucking chaplain! Go beat on him!" Olmstead pointed towards Lyman.

"I don't want to get anywhere near that asshole!" Silas replied, eyeing Lyman suspiciously.

"Neither do I," Wilkes announced, surprising everyone by cocking back the hammer on his pistol and firing a bullet directly through the chaplain's skull. A mist of black blood followed the bullet out of Lyman's head. His body crumpled to the ground and lay still.

"Jesus Christ, Captain," Zollenger muttered.

"Thanks to the quick thinking of Sergeant Armington, we know that fire kills this shit, whatever it is," Wilkes started, swinging his attention around the camp to make sure everybody was hearing him. "Gather up all the bodies and burn them. Including this son of a bitch right here." Wilkes kicked his boot into Lyman's body, forcing the chaplain's body to roll face up. "And don't forget to include that puddle of shit over there that used to be Private Dalton."

"Yes, sir!" the men in gray all snapped to attention in unison and began bustling around in deference to their orders

Even I played my part. My hands now free, I helped the men drag the bodies to the flickering flames.

******

The Dalton puddle taken care of, we sat and watched as the rest of the bodies roasted on the open fire. It didn't take long to realize that we had a problem, however.

"Sir…" I was standing by Singleton's side as he made the report to his captain, nervously wringing his cap in his hands. "The bodies are all on the fire, burning as instructed, except…"

"Go on, Private," Wilkes prodded.

"Well, sir, the chaplain…"

"Yes?" Wilkes was growing impatient.

"It doesn't seem to be burning, sir."

Wilkes sat closemouthed as he digested the private's words. Then: "Impossible!" Wilkes flew up from where he was sitting and made a beeline for the fire.

"First Sergeant!" Wilkes addressed Colt, who was standing near the fire, watching it burn away the bodies.

Colt snapped to attention when he realized the captain was talking to him. "Yes, sir?"

"Would you please remove the chaplain's body from the flames?"

"Yes, sir!" he responded, looking for the best place to grab without getting burned. He found one of Lyman's feet sticking out, as yet untouched by the flame. He grabbed the foot and tugged the body out of the inferno. He turned it so that Lyman was facing upwards.

Wilkes let his eyes wander the corpse. Lyman's clothing was mostly burned away, revealing his pinkish body. Despite having been in the flames for some time, the chaplain's flesh looked untouched, as if the fire had been nothing more than sunlight on a breezy summer day.

"Well, I'll be damned," Wilkes grumbled.

As we stared at Lyman's scarred face, it became obvious that the bullet hole in his forehead was slowly closing.

"I have to disagree, Captain. Fuck damned! We're all just straight up fucked!" Zollenger's booming voice argued. He had brought himself over to where everybody was congregating and must have spotted the same cruel reality as the rest of us.

"Sir?" Singleton called from behind Wilkes, having followed him over to the burning corpses. "What would you like us to do?"

Wilkes thought on it quietly. After a moment, he slowly started shaking his head. "I'll admit, Private, I don't have a damned clue. I'm fairly certain, though, that we don't want to be around when that hole in his head finishes healing up."

"Sir, I may have an idea." We all turned toward the speaker, Private McCarthy. McCarthy had ran to his tent when Tuttle's head had given way for the tentacle, and it had taken a long while before Zollenger and been able to coax the man to emerge. When the sergeant major accused him of cowardice, McCarthy had simply responded, "I'm just the cook." A look of disgust had crossed his expression and I hadn't seen Zollenger talk to the man since.

"What's your plan, Private?" Wilkes asked.

"Well, sir, there's gotta be a river nearby somewhere. I heard it off and on throughout our march yesterday. Maybe we could tie him up and dump him in. If he don't burn, maybe he'll drown?"

"What are you? Some kind of retard or something?" Olmstead screamed out at the private. Apparently, he had gathered himself enough to return to the land of the functioning. "If he comes back up alive, he'll just swim out!"

"Hey, fuck you, Olmstead!" Singleton screamed back, coming to the defense of the reserved McCarthy. "You're the reason we're in this mess, you and your fucking disregard for the rules. Stay the hell away from me, you diseased fuck!"

"Fuck you, you fucking cunt! I'll get as close to you as I like!" Olmstead yelled, starting to move towards McCarthy. He was stopped by Zollenger's cocked pistol jumping into his face.

"No you will not, Private Olmstead!" Zollenger warned. "In fact, you're going to stay at least ten paces away from everybody in this cursed camp until we get to where we're going, or I'll put a bullet through your brain pan. Are we clear, son?"

Olmstead looked defiant, but stepped back from the weapon. His eyes flashed over to Wilkes looking for sympathy. "Captain? You going to let him do this?"

Wilkes stood stone-faced, glaring at Olmstead. "As far as I'm concerned, you're still quarantined. Now, even more so." He turned to Zollenger. "Make it so, Sergeant Major," he announced with a pat on Zollenger's shoulder. The sergeant major shot a teasing smile at Olmstead.

Olmstead's shoulders slumped and he stepped back the required ten paces, sarcastically counting each one out aloud. "One…two…three…" Once Olmstead was out to ten, Wilkes spoke again.

"Now, Private Olmstead, if you don't like Private McCarthy's suggestion, what do you suggest?

"I say we shove Singleton's shotty right up between the good chaplain's butt cheeks and blow his goddamn brain out through his asshole!"

Eyes rolled throughout the camp. All except Silas'.

 "That's actually not a bad idea."

The entirety of the camp turned towards Silas, incredulity on their faces.

"I don't mean the ass part," Silas corrected with an annoyed glance towards Olmstead. "But a round or two from that shotgun would pretty much liquefy his head. I imagine it would take quite some time to come back from that, if he comes back at all.

"Perhaps we could do both; blow his head off and *then* drown him. Unless I got turned around on our course somewhere, I believe our survey maps of this area indicated that we should be coming upon a rather large river soon. Half a day's hike at the most. We tie him to something large to make sure he stays under, just to be extra safe."

Wilkes looked curiously at Silas. "Survey maps, huh? Our course? You some kind of orienteer, Sergeant?"

Silas smiled sheepishly. "Yes, sir. Been orienteering since I was just a wee lad. That's why I have come up the ranks as quickly as I have.

I am a helluva guide, sir." He smile was much less sheepish by the time he finished.

At least I now knew why Silas had bothered to hide away his compass when he had been captured, though I still didn't know what to consider *where* he had hidden it.

"Half a day, you say?"

Silas nodded. "Thereabouts, sir."

Wilkes bit his lip as he pondered the information.

"Uh, guys?" I cut in while Wilkes was thinking over his next move. I instinctively reached behind myself to slap the nearest person's hand. That person ended up being Silas.

"What is it, Winny?"

"The hole!" I said, pointing at the chaplain. "It's almost completely sealed."

Silas looked over at the chaplain's corpse and saw it as well. "Shit! He's right."

"Private Singleton," Wilkes called out. "Would you kindly bring your shotgun over to us? With haste, please."

"Yes, sir." Singleton ran off and quickly returned with the shotgun. Before Singleton could hand it over to Wilkes, Silas swiped it from him and aimed it at the chaplain's head.

Just in time, as it turned out. No sooner had he gotten the barrel pointed, than Lyman's eyes shot open. Silas didn't hesitate. He pulled the trigger, releasing its thunderous roar into the tranquil forest. Just as quickly as Lyman's eyes had flung open, his entire head disappeared. Nothing but a red pool remained, its crimson sheen only broken by white shards of skull.

The momentary silence that followed was broken by the orders of Captain Wilkes. "Alright, men. Pack up and carry what you can. We're moving out. Private Olmstead, as far as I'm concerned, you've volunteered yourself to carry the chaplain's body until we hit this river that the sergeant spoke of."

CHAPLAIN

Olmstead looked ready to argue, but one glance over at Zollenger, who was menacingly tapping his now-holstered pistol, gave him second thoughts. Instead, he just nodded.

"Let's be quick!" Wilkes continued. "Much daylight has already burned and we've got quite a distance yet to travel."

******

Silas was indeed a gifted orienteer. True to his word, we reached the river soon after the sun had crested and began its long journey down to the western horizon.

The day's trek had provided me with many occasions to grin. Whenever I would look towards Olmstead, who marched several paces forward of us the entire time, I would see him nervously glancing back at the tattered flesh of the chaplain's throat. I think that he assumed a tentacle was going to sprout out at any moment and consume his arrogant head.

That didn't happen.

In truth, I had been expecting to see the chaplain's head slowly reform itself as we journeyed. First the chin, then the mouth, cheeks, and ears. The nose next, then the eyes. All the way until a complete head had regrown atop those lanky shoulders and his cackle once again emerging to send shivers down my spine.

Thankfully, that hadn't happened either.

Having seen no signs of regeneration by the time we hit the river, the men in the troop were breathing a little easier. The chaplain appeared to be dead...for real this time! Still, we stuck to the original plan and searched for something to sink him with.

As Silas had earlier said...just to be safe!

We considered tying him to a heavy tree branch, as there were plenty of those around, but we decided that it would take far too long to get waterlogged and sink to the bottom. We wanted the chaplain buried in his watery grave as soon as possible.

Finally, we settled on a large boulder sticking up just at the bank of the river. It had to way a ton at least, but still having nine men left - including myself - we figured there'd be enough strength between us to shove the boulder into the water. Using several long lengths of rope, we secured the chaplain's body to the river-facing side of the boulder. Zollenger made sure that the rope was as tight as possible. "Why take any chances?" he offered as explanation.

Once everyone was satisfied that the job had been done well enough, we all huddled at the large rock and began pushing. At first, it didn't budge. We kept pushing, but I could tell that several of the men were already gearing to give up on this plan, when the boulder finally gave and slid ever-so-slightly forward through the mud of the bank. This encouraged the men, who pushed again with renewed strength.

Finally, after what felt like hours, the boulder dropped off the embankment and landed with a loud splash in the water. It tipped onto its side when it hit, the side that the chaplain's body was on, making the men smile when they realized that the boulder was going to end up lying atop the corpse, pinning it to the river's floor.

With that done, we took a quick break to catch our breath and fill our canteens. From upstream, of course. Then we left that cursed resting place of the damned and journeyed on.

We traveled for a long while, continuing even after the sun had disappeared from the sky, though nobody complained. Everybody just wanted to get as far away from all that had happened that day as possible.

That night, in a tent all to myself, I had no trouble sleeping at all.

July 9ᵗʰ, 1863

I awoke the next morning feeling more rested than I had in days. A stretch and a yawn later, I stood, letting my blankets crumple to the floor. Shaking off the last vestiges of sleep, I made my way outside into the brisk morning air.

"Morning, Winny," Silas greeted, sipping hot brew by the fire. "Sleep well?"

I nodded. "I did. Very well, actually. You?"

Silas took another sip and then shook his head. "No. I can't say that *I* did. Too much on my mind, I suppose." His eyes held a far-away look to them, most likely peering into the past day's events.

McCarthy approached me, extending a steaming mug and a metal bowl. "Breakfast?" he offered. I nodded and gladly took both items. The meal wasn't much - just bacon and toast - but the coffee was good. I took a sip and thanked the portly man. McCarthy smiled and sauntered off to prepare more of the morning's rations.

I took a few moments to myself and my meal. It had been many days since I had been able to enjoy the freedom of...well...freedom! I took in the nearby sounds of the forest. Birds chirping. The rush of the river just beyond the surrounding trees. I was experiencing some queer elixir of peace and exhilaration.

Judging by the face of the men slowly rising around me, I was the only one enjoying such emotions. The benefits of a young psyche's ability to remain flexible, I guessed. The men, if anything, seemed to be even more morose than the day before.

Except Olmstead. Sitting off by himself, back against a tree stump, he was smiling up into the sky. His nearest company that of Holton, digging into a similar metal bowl. Holton's rifle was perched across his lap as he ate, its barrel left pointing in Olmstead's general direction. Holton must have drawn the guard duty again.

McCarthy rounded the fire, carrying a new offering of breakfast towards Olmstead. His stride slow, filled with trepidation the closer he got to the segregated man.

"That asshole's funk sure didn't last long," Silas spoke up, noticing the direction of my gaze. "The sheer amount of hot air coming out of his mouth nearly set my ass to scalding last night."

"Did you have to watch after him?" I asked, surprised.

Silas nodded. "Yeah. I split last night's watch with Corporal Holton," he explained. "Somebody had to do it. Pain in the ass, but much better being the watch*er* than the watch*ee*, I suppose."

McCarthy's steps had grown very sporadic by the time he neared Olmstead, as if he feared that a giant flesh-eating tentacle would come ripping out of the man's skull at any moment. Justifiably so, I reckoned. The metal dishes in his hands were clearly shaking.

Olmstead smiled up towards McCarthy, his eyes glued on the cook as he slowly extended the dishes towards him. Olmstead had remained calmly slouched until McCarthy was within arm's reach, then suddenly sprang his upper body forward, yelling "Boo!"

McCarthy pounced backward with the quickness of a startled cat. The dishes spilled from his hands and crashed onto the grass of the forest floor. The man himself landed hard on his ass with a crack, but immediately scrambled backwards several feet.

Olmstead fell back laughing. "You fucking fat moron," Olmstead chuckled. He continued laughing until his eyes caught on the metal bowl, now lying face down in the dirt. He whipped out his leg, kicking the bowl towards McCarthy. "Way to go! You done gone and spilled my breakfast!"

McCarthy didn't respond, just laid back where he had landed, quaking in fear.

"Boy, you some kind of special, ain't ya?" Olmstead continued, the smile dropping from his face. "You remind me of my sister's retard cousin."

Still nothing but whimpers from McCarthy.

Olmstead got visibly angry and reached out to snatch up the metal bowl, which he then frisbee'd towards McCarthy, the metal clanging against the cook's forehead. "Go get me another bowl, dipshit!" he yelled.

A loud crack split the morning, a patch of dirt spouting up from next to Olmstead's knees. All eyes shifted to Sergeant Major Zollenger, who had just fired the warning shot towards Olmstead. "Boy, I will abide your attitude no longer! I won't hesitate to put a bullet in ya if you keep acting up, you got me?" Zollenger warned.

"I got ya, Sergeant Major," Olmstead reluctantly confirmed. "I's just hungry is all."

"Well, tough shit!" Zollenger spat. "Looks like you'll be starving until lunchtime. And that's only if Private McCarthy decides to be generous and prepare a serving for you." Zollenger reached out and helped McCarthy back to his feet. "I personally won't be requiring him to do so," Zollenger spoke; the words intended for Olmstead, but directed at McCarthy as he brushed the dirt off him.

Olmstead momentarily stared at Zollenger, hatred burning in his eyes, until he eventually relented and resumed his slouching position against the small stump.

＊＊＊＊＊＊

Our march had slowed much from the rigorous pace of days past. Trepidation hung thick as the previous day's events finally caught up with the men, their adrenaline having waned from the encounter with the black beast. Still, *ever forward* was Captain Wilkes' mantra.

"I was thinking," I spoke, walking by Silas' side, "I could take a watch on Olmstead tonight. Lessen the load for you and Corporal Holton."

"I don't know if that's a good idea, Winny," Silas answered, shaking his head.

"I'll be okay. My daddy taught me how to use a rifle early on as a boy."

"It's more than that. If he does something foolish – which he'll likely be more inclined to do if he sees it's *you* watching him - you may have to actually use that rifle on him. I doubt that'd be an easy thing for a boy so young."

"I ain't *that* young!" I protested. "I'll be ten in October."

Silas chuckled. "That's pretty young from where I'm standing."

"Come on," I pleaded. "I can do it. It's not like I like the guy. I rather despise him, actually. I wouldn't have any problem putting a bullet through him if the situation called upon me to do so."

Silas studied me for a moment.

"Now, I'm not saying he will – there's no signs indicating that that black shit did anything to him as of yet - but what if he ends up like Tuttle, or even Dalton?" he asked. "What then?"

"I'd shoot him first, then raise the alarm."

Silas laughed. "Sounds about right," he conceded. "I'll bring it up to Captain Wilkes. See what he thinks."

I smirked and shook a fist of victory in the air.

******

"Well shit," Zollenger's voice called out from in front of us. He had taken it upon himself to stand as Olmstead's guard, gun trained on the arrogant man's back. Olmstead was being forced to take point in our march, careful to stay at least ten paces to the front of the procession at all times. "It looks like we're going to have to cross!" the master sergeant yelled back to us.

Continuing up to where Zollenger was standing, we broke out from the trees to see the river blocking our path. The dry land ended at the river bank as the water wound its way to, and then along, the base of a cliff.

Zollenger set his knapsack on the ground and pulled his canteen out for a sip. "We'll need to cross here to continue on," he informed taking another sip. "The water looks shallow enough; the current mild. We should be okay," he judged.

I gulped. We were going to cross this thing? I fought down a panic attack as my eyes followed the current of the river. I frantically searched around for a way around the river, but I couldn't see any other choice.

"Wait a minute!" Olmstead exclaimed. "Is this the same fucking river that we dropped the chaplain into?"

Everyone turned to Silas.

"It is," he confirmed with a nod. "It's traveling the same way as us. We'll most likely be following right along it for the next couple days. Maybe more."

"That's just fucking fantastic!" Olmstead griped. To be fair, though, I could hear the rest of the men grumbling right along with him.

"For once, I agree with you Olmstead," Zollenger responded. "And you know what the fantastic part is? The fantastic part is, if there *is* anything in that water, you'll be the first to find out," the sergeant major chortled.

A small tremor ran through Olmstead's body. "You gonna make me cross first?"

"You're damn right I am!" Zollenger asserted. "But don't worry your skinny little breeches none, Sally. I'll be in there with ya,...gun aimed right at your back."

Olmstead didn't look to be comforted by this revelation.

"After all, I wouldn't let one of my men do something that I myself, was not willing to do." Zollenger winked at Olmstead and hefted his large knapsack back over his shoulders.

"Alright, listen up!" Wilkes stepped forward. "This is how we're going to do this! Sergeant Major and Private Olmstead will cross first, making sure there are no unpleasant surprises awaiting us in that water. Once they are safely across, the rest of us will follow single file." He looked around to make sure everybody was paying attention. "Keep a careful eye on the man in front of you, so they don't get swept away. Remember, Hell's denizens aren't the only concern here." The men nodded. "Private McCarthy, you'll be the first to cross after we get the go-ahead from the sergeant major." McCarthy reluctantly nodded. "Then you, Private Singleton. Sergeant Armington, I'm concerned about the boy. He's the smallest among us and could get carried away easily."

"I've got him," Silas assured.

"Good. Then you and the boy will go next. Corporal Holton will follow them up, then myself. First Sergeant Colt, being the largest man here, I'll expect you to cross last, watching our rear."

"Easy day, sir," Colt acknowledged with a grin.

"Okay, let's do this," Wilkes announced.

"Time to pucker up, pretty!" Zollenger teased, gesturing the barrel of his rifle towards the rushing water.

I could see that Olmstead wanted to defy Zollenger, but, realizing it would be a futile effort, he let his shoulders fall limp and trudged to the water's edge. "It's a hot day anyway. I was just thinking that I could go for a quick dip," he announced, attempting to save as much face as he could, before stepping into the water and slowly wading into its depths.

Zollenger let Olmstead get a few steps in, and then followed. He kept his eyes, and gun, posted on Olmstead's back as he made his way into the flowing brook.

We all watched the crossing intently. Everyone was on edge, just waiting for something untoward to happen. The two men crossed slowly, carefully weighing each step to ensure that the water's grip wasn't able to take hold. Reaching the middle, Olmstead held his arms out over his shoulders, both to maintain his balance, and to keep them from being immersed in the water that had risen to his breast-line. Soon after, he rose up out of the water on the other bank. Zollenger quickly followed, and, with both men back on dry ground, the camp let out the collective breath that they had been holding.

"Good to go!" Zollenger yelled out over the river. "Turns out she's easier to cross than a redhead!"

McCarthy looked un-consoled by the previous successful crossing as he hefted his two large packs onto his back; one his personal knapsack, and the other holding the dwindling rations and cooking gear for the troops. He admirably balanced the bags as he haltingly stepped into the river, each step bringing a fear-filled wince.

Singleton followed, and then it was our turn. "You ready for this?" Silas asked me, likely judging my nervous shaking.

"I'm not a big fan of water, but I'll do my best." Silas shot me a worried glance. "I'm sure I'll be fine," I tried assuring him, though the words fell flat of even assuring myself.

"I'll keep a good grip on your shirt as we cross. If I start to feel you slipping, I'll grab you up. Deal?"

I nodded. "Deal."

It would have to do.

We crept out into the water, the river's chill a stark contrast to the warm mugginess of the woods. I concentrated on firmly planting my foot in the loose muck of the riverbed. One step, then the next, then the next; one after the other.

"I spoke with Captain Wilkes earlier, and he okayed you standing the watch this evening," Silas related.

I was happy for the distraction and nodded my appreciation.

I must say, I was handling myself quite well; at least until we finally dipped into the depths of the river's center, the water level rising to engulf my shoulders. The water's momentum caused it to lap onto my face as it sped by, inducing my anxiety as the cold liquid worked its way up my nose, mimicking the sensation of drowning.

Silas must have sensed my panic kicking in. His grip tightened and he leaned into my ear. "I've got you…I've got you," he repeated, his voice smooth and calming. I clamped my eyelids shut and forced myself to once more concentrate on moving my legs forward. One step, then the next. After what seemed like hours - though in reality was only a few seconds - the water finally started to recede down my body, first freeing my shoulders then my chest. With every inch the water crawled downward, my anxiety sank to match its plunge.

I opened my eyes and saw that Singleton was passing up McCarthy, who was very slowly picking his way forward through the water now down at his waist. "You doing alright, McCarthy?" Singleton asked as he reached him.

McCarthy nodded his head. "Yeah, I-I'm o-okay," he stuttered, most likely from both the cold of the water and the fear he was experiencing.

Singleton nodded back at him and continued forward. He hadn't gotten more than five steps away when McCarthy screamed and crashed forward into the water. The ration bag came loose from his shoulders, and I could only watch as it was carried away with the river's current.

"It's got me!" McCarthy screamed, flailing wildly in the stream. Water filled his gaping mouth, blocking another scream, but McCarthy spit it out and continued shouting. "It's fucking got me!"

Singleton spun towards the commotion, but was too shocked to make any attempt at rescue. Silas, however, sprung directly into action. He let go of me and charged forward towards McCarthy. He threw himself into the thrashing man and they both briefly disappeared into the water's maw. Lots of splashing erupted from the position they had gone under and I would only get short glimpses of their bodies as the underwater wrestling continued.

Silas was the first to emerge from the roiling water, standing on his own two feet. He reached down and violently smacked McCarthy across the face. "Stop it!" he yelled to accompany the open-handed assault. "Get ahold of yourself!" Silas held a matted green net up to McCarthy's face, letting the wild man's eyes focus in on it. "Look! It's just river weeds!" He shoved the mat in closer. It took another moment, but McCarthy's thrashing finally started to die down as his mind caught up with what Silas was showing him.

His nerves finally being wrested back under his control, McCarthy asked, "River weeds?"

"Yes. River weeds," Silas answered, once again shaking the green mat in front of McCarthy's face. "From the river bed. Your legs got caught up in it."

McCarthy relaxed as the reality of his impending non-death clarified in his mind. "River weeds," he said again, taking the mat from Silas and letting it fall back into the water.

A loud burst of laughter erupted from the approaching shoreline. I looked up to see Olmstead hysterically chuckling. "Ha ha! River weeds! You fat, moronic piece of shit!" Olmstead held his gut and fell to his knees from laughing so hard. "River weeds!? Ha ha ha!"

He continued snickering, all the way until he was silenced by the butt of Zollenger's rifle smashing into his nose. "Keep quiet, shit bird!" Zollenger chastised.

The force of the strike knocked Olmstead onto his ass. "What the fuck, Sergeant Major!? Was that really necessary?" Olmstead whined after getting past the initial bout of dizziness.

Zollenger never answered the challenge, however. He was too busy staring at the blood leaking from Olmstead's smashed nose.

It was black.

******

The remainder of the unit crossed the river without further incident. Zollenger had moved Olmstead further from the rushing water, attempting to keep the men from noticing the black ooze that had leaked from his broken nose. It worked, as the men were calmly lying around on the bank, letting the sun's heat work to dry their soaked uniforms.

All except McCarthy, who was stewing with tears in his eyes. He looked up at Wilkes as the captain was walking by him.

"I'm sorry, sir. I lost the bag containing our rations," McCarthy explained, shame in his eyes.

"Nothing we can do about it now, Private." Wilkes gave McCarthy's shoulder a reassuring squeeze. "Maybe we'll come across it as we move further down the river."

McCarthy's eyes lit a little as he considered the possibility. "Maybe so, sir. I'll keep an eye out for it."

"You do that, Private," Wilkes finished, stepping away while removing his dripping blouse.

"I've spotted some blackberries growing around here, sir. I'll gather some up so we have something to eat tonight," McCarthy promised.

"Good idea, Private. Make it happen." Wilkes smiled at the cook as he ran off to take care of business.

"Captain Wilkes," Zollenger quietly called out once Wilkes was in reasonable earshot.

"Yes, Sergeant Major?" Wilkes replied, wringing his blouse out over the muddy bank.

"Could you come over here real quick, sir? I've got something you'll want to see."

Wilkes slowly made his way over to Zollenger, working himself back into his still-dripping blouse. "What is it, Sergeant Major?"

Once he was near, Zollenger stepped out from between Olmstead and the captain. Wilkes' eyes widened when he saw the black smudge spread over Olmstead's nose. Olmstead sat perfectly still, scared out of his wits at what the sergeant major's gun butt had revealed.

"What are we going to do with him, sir?" Zollenger asked.

Wilkes mulled it over for a moment, then reached into his pocket and withdrew a soaked neckerchief. He tossed the sopping fabric into Olmstead's lap. "Clean yourself up, soldier." He turned towards Zollenger. "I don't want to unnecessarily spook the troops."

"Just give the word, sir, and I can shoot this asshole in the head and set him ablaze," Zollenger suggested.

Wilkes studied Olmstead's pleading eyes. "Not just yet, Sergeant Major. We don't have the first clue as to how this infection – or whatever it is - works. It doesn't sit well with me, killing our own when we aren't sure. We'll keep him with us until we make it back to proper society and can hand him over to the docs. Maybe they can make something out of all this."

"Thank you, sir," Olmstead elated, though he did so keeping as still and quiet as possible to avoid tempting the twitchy trigger finger of the sergeant major.

"Make no mistake though, Private," Wilkes leaned down and stared directly into Olmstead's eyes, "I will not hesitate to shoot you myself if you make one move that I don't agree with. Something as small as crossing your feet to a tumble, or even breathing in a foul way, and I'll put you down! Got it?"

"Got it, sir."

"Good. From here on out, you are on the shortest leash ever crafted," Wilkes warned, stepping away. He stopped after a couple paces and turned to Zollenger. "Obviously, the quarantine still stands. Keep him away from the other troops."

"Of course, sir!" Zollenger responded.

I finished my business in the bush that I had eavesdropped from and stepped back out into the crowd. I did my best to bite back the dismay roiling in my gut from the captain's decision.

******

Wilkes decided to not have us travel much further that day. We walked into the cover of the trees and set up camp only a couple hundred yards from the bank. Mainly due to the men feeling uncomfortable being so near the water and what it may contain.

True to his word, McCarthy had gathered a large number of berries, which were distributed out to the men. Blackberries and raspberries, mostly.

As soon as night fell, I had grabbed a handful of berries, placed them in a small sack, and retreated to my tent. I wanted to get an early start on my sleep, as I knew that I'd be awoken early for my volunteered guard duty. Curled in my wool blankets, I ended up barely touching the berries before drifting off into the majesty of sleep.

July 10ᵗʰ, 1863

I awoke to my ankle being shaken.

"Winny," I heard through the darkness of my eyelids. "Winny, time to wake." The shaking persisted.

I slowly opened my eyes, forcing myself from the heavy bog of sleep.

I looked down to see Silas was the source of the incessant shaking. "It's time for your shift," he informed once he saw that he had my awakened attention.

I groaned.

"Hey, *you* asked for it," he joked.

I crawled out of the warmth of my blankets into the chilly mountain air. "What time is it?" I asked, rubbing my eyes.

"About an hour 'til sunrise," he informed.

"What?" I asked, astonished. "Weren't you suppose to wake me a couple hours ago?"

Silas shrugged. "I've been feeling fine and decided to keep the watch a little longer. Besides, it being your first watch, I figured I'd cut you a break."

I was a little annoyed, but seeing as how rising from sleep had already felt like trying to climb out of quicksand, I didn't argue. Quite the opposite. "Well, a thank you is in order, I suppose."

"You're welcome." Silas smiled. "I'm gonna go grab a bit of shut eye, so have fun. Remember, keep your eyes open and don't listen to a word that prick says. He's been out for a couple hours now, but I'm sure he'll try to rile you up when he awakes. Just ignore whatever comes out of his mouth and you should be alright."

I nodded. "Will do."

"You sure you don't want me to stick around?" he asked, concerned.

"Nah," I replied. "I've got this."

Silas started heading away, but turned at the last minute. "Also, a pot of coffee is on the fire if you need some."

"Thanks!" I said to Silas' back. I watched as he disappeared into the shadows near his tent.

I glanced over to Olmstead and saw that he was sleeping, so I stepped over to the fire and poured myself a mug of the steamy brew. I needed it that morning.

I took the scalding liquid over to a nice perch about fifteen paces from the sleeping form of Olmstead. He was lied out at the base of a boulder, snug in a pile of blankets.

I sat still, letting my eyes wander the camp; as best as I could see it in the pervading darkness, that is. I kept the gun laid across my lap and bit back the excitement of what I was doing. It wasn't official - and I suppose that you could say that I was serving for the wrong color of uniform - but I was standing a military watch, and that had me charged.

It wasn't long before the blackness of the sky began to brighten. The sky was just a tinge brighter – a drowned navy blue in color – when the first stirrings of camp reached my ears. My eyes searched until I identified the initial source of the commotion.

McCarthy exited his tent, stretching his arms out into a wide vee and yawning. He stumbled over to the fire, checking the coffee pot there, then rubbed his hands together over the flame's blessed heat.

Olmstead turned a little in his sleep. A quick inspection revealed he was still out, just having stirred some.

"Winny, right?" McCarthy's voice caused me to jump. He had left the fire behind and was slowly approaching me.

"It is," I answered.

With a yawn, "I'm going to go back over to the river bed and gather some more berries for breakfast this morning. I'll be back soon, in case anybody is asking."

"You do that then, you fat bastard." I startled and my hand instinctively tightened around the rifle's grip. It was Olmstead, stretching out and then raising himself from his prone position, until his back was resting against the boulder.

McCarthy scowled at the waking man and stormed off, vanishing into the trees. Olmstead's eyes followed the cook as he disappeared from sight.

"How he found is way out of his mama's snatch I will never know," Olmstead muttered, finishing with a loud yawn. It was then that he seemed to notice me for the first time.

"What the fuck is this!?" he asked, his boisterous volume seeming much louder in the peaceful quiet of the morning. "Now they got a damn kid watching me?"

"What of it?" I challenged.

Olmstead regarded me with a curious stare. "Nothing, I reckon." He slouched against the boulder and actually managed to be silent for a couple moments.

Of course, that didn't last.

"Tell you what, kid. You don't like me much, I can tell that. I ain't no idiot like that fat mess cook out there in dem woods right now. And I'm not too fond of being a prisoner in my own army, neither." I stayed silent, not seeing what his point was. "So, how's about you let me just walk out of here? I promise not to fuss with nothing on my way out. I'll just up and leave you all be. You'll never have to see me again. How does that sound?"

I intentionally planted the butt of the rifle into the ground at my side, barrel facing skyward, for visual effect to support my reply. "You do that, and I'll blow off your balls from here to Lincoln's lap. How does that sound?" I grinned.

Olmstead actually laughed. "You is a tough-talking little shit, ain't ya?" He hooted and clapped his hands together.

I sat silently, choosing to deny him the pleasure of a response. Instead, I let my gaze bore into him. Realizing this, Olmstead decided to provoke further.

"You fancy yourself as some sort of little badass, don't ya?"

I remained mum, remembering Silas' words of caution.

"Not biting, huh?" Olmstead poked. "I suppose maybe your fancy is warranted. Good job, kid."

A compliment?

"When all of this is over, I'm going to have to go out and find the bitch that bore ya. She must be one helluva woman!"

My grip tightened slightly on the rifle, but I continued biting my tongue. I had always been protective of my mother; once even giving a fellow classmate a bloody nose following a particularly cruel comment about her. Of course, despite my noble intentions, my father had beat my ass plenty when he had heard about that.

"I'm sure any cunt that births a bad ass like you would feel real nice wrapped around my pecker!"

My resolve didn't crumble; *vaporized* would be a more accurate description. I hefted the rifle and started to jump up. I'm not sure what my play was going to be, but, luckily, I never had to find out. A hand reached from behind me and gripped tight on my shoulder, stopping my leap as soon as it had begun.

"Easy, Winny," I heard Silas' soft tone behind me. "He isn't worth it."

I looked back into the concerned face of Silas and let my emotions succumb back within my control.

"He's just trying to get you to do something stupid," Silas further explained.

Eventually, I nodded and let myself settle back to the ground. Returning my glare to Olmstead, I saw that he now wore a look of disappointment.

"Fuck it," he griped. "I'm going to catch some more sleep." He lowered himself back into a prone position and was lost under his blankets.

"Thanks," I murmured back to Silas. "Though I thought you were going to catch some sleep?"

"Nah," Silas replied. "I figured I'd watch your back with this one. I doubt you've had much experience with a son of a bitch like him before."

I was a bit annoyed at the lack of trust, but it turned out he hadn't been wrong. I thanked him again.

"Anyway, I'm going to grab another mug. You want some?" I nodded and handed him my cup, which he carried with him over to the fire.

In the silence that followed, I heard a sound; slight, almost lost in the surrounding foliage. It came from deep in the distance. I couldn't be sure, but it sounded like someone screaming.

******

The sun rose and the men of the camp soon followed, congregating around the camp fire.

"Alright, men," Wilkes broadcasted as he joined the group surrounding the fire. "The usual drill. 30 minutes. Warm up, eat some chow, and get your gear ready to go."

"Speaking of chow, where in the hell is McCarthy?" First Sergeant Colt asked, scanning the camp ground for any signs of the mess cook.

"Don't ask me," Holton shrugged when Colt' gaze fell onto him. 'I haven't seen him all morning."

Zollenger rolled his eyes. "For the love of shit, where did that boy get off to?"

"Excuse me, Sergeant Major," I called out, getting Zollenger's attention. "He left earlier this morning, saying he was going back to the river to grab more berries for the breakfast."

"Did he now?" Zollenger asked, stroking his bearded chin. He turned back to the men at the fire. "Holton!"

"Yes, Sergeant Major!" Holton popped up from his sitting spot.

"Go down to the river bank and find our wayward cook please. See if he needs any help," Zollenger ordered.

Holton immediately rushed off towards the tree line.

"Corporal!" Zollenger called after him, stopping him before he disappeared. Holton turned back to the sergeant major. "Take Private Singleton with you. Just to be safe."

Singleton took his queue and jumped up to join Holton. Once together, both men vanished into the trees.

"Well, might as well pack while we're waiting for breakfast to show up," Colt reasoned while taking a sip from his mug. He set the cup down and left the glow of the fire to stow his gear. The remaining men split to do the same.

Fifteen minutes passed, and the men had finished packing. Once again they were around the fire, now growing tense.

"Where the hell are they?" Zollenger asked nobody in particular.

Soon, a rustling from the trees announced the arrival of the two searchers. Holton and Singleton both ran back into the camp clearing.

"Sergeant Major!" Holton called out. He let his feet carry him the rest of the way up to Zollenger. "Sergeant Major," he said again, short of breath. "We couldn't find McCarthy."

"What?" Zollenger asked.

"He wasn't on the riverbank," Holton explained.

"We searched up and down along the river for a while, then combed through the surrounding trees, as well," Singleton cut in. "Nothing, Sergeant Major. No sign of him."

"Fuck!" Zollenger screamed into the mountain air.

"Calm yourself, Sergeant Major," Wilkes ordered softly. "We don't know anything yet."

Zollenger took a deep breath, then turned back to his captain. "What're your orders, sir?"

Wilkes mulled it over for a moment, then: "I think we'll delay our departure for a bit. See if he shows up."

"Are you sure, sir?" Colt challenged. "What if it's that thing we threw in the river?" Colt was now refusing to even acknowledge the chaplain as a man.

Nobody offered to correct him.

"Like I said, we know nothing at this point," Wilkes reinforced. "Let's wait a bit and see if he shows. We're not going to leave a man behind just because we are scared."

Colt glared at the captain for a moment, but soon backed down, resigning himself to another cup of coffee.

Olmstead woke again with a yawn. He looked around the camp, noticing the pale faces of his compatriots. "Y'all look like you just saw some ghost titties?" Olmstead laughed until he noticed that nobody was paying his quip any attention.

The camp settled in for the wait.

******

The sun was high in the sky by the time Zollenger whispered into Wilkes' ear. "Sir, we're losing daylight. We need to either start marching soon, or make plans to wait it out here for the night."

Wilkes stared off, working through his internal conundrum. "I'm not comfortable leaving a man behind, Sergeant Major. We'll wait it out tonight. If there is no sign of him by morning, we'll move on without him."

Zollenger nodded, though he didn't look to agree with his superior.

"I know what you want to say. I don't like staying put, either," Wilkes sympathized. "That damn river gives me the chills."

"Yes, sir," Zollenger agreed.

"You a hunter, Sergeant Major?" Wilkes asked.

Zollenger was caught off guard by the question, but nodded. "Since I was a boy."

"Good." Wilkes turned and shouted out to the men. "Listen up! Sergeant Armington, you and Sergeant Major are going to go out and see if you can bag us something to eat. First Sergeant and Private Singleton you'll do the same. Corporal Holton, you and the boy will keep guard on our quarantined private." Wilkes looked over at me. "You up for that, Winny?"

I nodded.

"Three things," he yelled out, turning back towards the rest of the men. "One, keep your eyes peeled for Private McCarthy. He's out there somewhere. If you find him, escort him back here." Wilkes pause. "Two, don't get lost yourselves. We're leaving in the morning, with or without you."

"And the third thing, sir?" Colt asked.

"The third thing is," Wilkes announced with a cold look, "keep away from that damned river."

******

The hunting party had only been successful at catching a couple rabbits. No big game and, more importantly, no sign of McCarthy.

The rabbits were split among all eight of us. Not a huge meal, but enough to silence our growling stomachs. Normally, the tough meat would have been entirely too gamey for my taste, but I devoured it all the same.

The mood around camp was bleak as night fell and we divided into our respective sleeping areas. I was weary from a long day that contained few bright spots during its tenure.

I did, however, manage a smile when I unrolled my blankets and found the previous night's sack of berries. I snacked on them until my eyelids drooped closed and sleep carried me off.

July 11ᵗʰ, 1863

I'm not sure what awoke me that night, but my eyes opened into the complete darkness of the tent. My hairs stood on end as I felt an untenable dread hanging thick in the air. Though the dread was not alone. It was hard to breathe, as the dew in the stifling air weighed heavy. It was hot and humid in a way I had not experienced outside of a bath house.

I blindly felt around until my fingers brushed the oil lamp. I seized the lamp and proceeded to light its wick. The orange light spread throughout the tent, causing the walls to flicker in shapes and shadows.

I sensed a presence with me inside the tent. I scanned around, but did not see anything out of place. While nothing sinister initially revealed itself, I could feel a malevolent presence nonetheless.

Then I heard it. From up above me. The sound of something wet slithering. I looked up at the roof of the tent and that is where my discomfort was confirmed.

My gut reaction told me to scream. To shout until my voice was hoarse. I did not, however. I tried – believe me I tried – but I could not manage more than a squeak to emerge from my lips.

Defying the laws of gravity, an inky puddle hung from the apex of the tent. The puddle expanded and contracted a couple times, then began to transform, shaping into three long tendrils that coiled in on themselves, as if they were black snakes communing in a nest. I watched the tendrils perform their perverse dance until their shape started to fade, melting, once again, into a loose puddle of black.

The puddle then started swirling around in a circular motion, much like a whirlpool. An inky finger emerged from the whirlpool's vortex. The finger slowly extended downwards towards me.

Again, I halfway tried screaming, but my voice was still frozen in my throat. The finger stopped its descent about between me and the swirling puddle.

I stared at the tip of the finger as it hung still in the air. I felt sure that it was also staring right back at me. After a moment of this speechless interaction, the finger's tip began pulling in on itself, coalescing into a thick blob hanging from a nub. The blob quickly melted into another shape...a shape I knew all too well.

The scarred visage of the chaplain stared at me with his typical sneer, his face having formed at the end of the long filament of blackness.

His eyes, themselves just a pool of black, regarded me intensely. Then he spoke.

"Boy!" The word came out harshly, stinging my soul like some kind of phantom wasp. "It's time to receive God's blessings."

I watched in horror as his face quickly melted back into the shapeless blob and then shot out at me. The sludge slapped wetly against my face, blocking all light and air. I felt as it wrapped itself around my entire skull.

Though the sound was unable to penetrate past the oily mass, I finally was able to scream.

******

I was still lost in the blackness when my foot started to shake. "Winny," I could hear from the darkness. "Winny!" The incessant shaking of my foot continued.

"Leave me alone!" I wanted to scream. Perhaps I did scream it...I wasn't sure.

"Winny, wake up!"

My eyes shot open. The flickering of fire light soaked through into my pupils. The black sludge was no longer covering my face. I quickly searched for the puddle of ooze at the top of the tent. It, too, was gone. No trace left behind that it had ever existed.

"Jesus Christ, boy! You scared me." The voice came from my shaking foot. It was Silas, shaking me awake in the same manner as the morning prior.

"You okay?" he concernedly asked. "Sounds like you were having one hell of a nightmare."

I searched around again, making absolutely sure that there was no sign of the oily demon.

"Yeah. I'm fine," I answered, once I was convinced that we were alone.

"Okay, then. You up for watching Olmstead? I wasn't planning on going back to sleep, if you don't feel up to it."

I thought about it. I was feeling a bit tired still, but I also no longer felt like being alone. I was scared.

"No, that's alright. I'll come out and sit with you though, if you don't mind." I crawled out from my blankets and made ready to follow Silas out of the tent. "I get to hold the gun, though!'

Silas laughed. "Yeah, Winny. No problem." He saw my face as it entered the light of his lamp and he mimed wiping at his lip. "Looks like you got a little berry juice left on your mouth." He shot me a knowing wink and pulled himself out of the tent.

I wiped a hand across my lips. They came away with a sticky, black smear. I hurriedly wiped my hand across my pants, ridding it of the ominous slime.

"It was from the blackberries. It was just the blackberries," I kept telling myself as I walked outside to join Silas.

******

Thankfully, Olmstead slept through the morning. Given my spooked state, I wasn't in the proper mood to deal with his barbaric attitude.

He slept soundly until Zollenger woke him with a kick to his boot. "Wake up, shit for brains. We're moving out in five."

Olmstead slowly lifted himself from the ground. He cleared his throat, spitting a nasty green glob into the grass.

"Five minutes? I'm fucking hungry," Olmstead griped. "Aren't we going to eat first?"

"We're all hungry. We'll keep on the lookout for something to eat as we're moving along," Zollenger explained. "Now be quick or get a bullet!"

We moved out, leaving that wretched campsite behind. Zollenger once again kept Olmstead at the front of the formation, gun to his back as before.

It wasn't much later that we came across a couple more rabbits, which Colt quickly shot and bagged up for lunch later in the day. We also came across some more berries, which the men all grabbed handfuls of, snacking on them as we marched.

After about three hours, we stopped briefly to feast on the rabbits, then moved on. Every so often, somebody in the party would call out into the trees for McCarthy. A response was never received.

"Well, isn't that just shit luck!" I heard from Olmstead up ahead. By this point, the sun was well on its way downwards and the men were growing weary.

"You've got to be fucking kidding me!" Zollenger joined in.

"What is it, Sergeant Major?" Wilkes asked, moving up to where Zollenger was standing.

"It's the river, sir. It takes another turn up here," Zollenger answered bleakly. "Looks like we're going to have to cross it again."

"Not again," I pleadingly whispered.

"Alright, gentlemen, you heard the sergeant major," Wilkes bellowed, "cinch your gear up tight for another crossing."

Grumbles erupted all around me.

"Well, I'll be covered in horse shit!" All eyes turned towards Holton. "Is that what I think it is?" he asked, pointing towards the river bank. We all followed his gesture. There, propped up against a tree and bobbing in the river's flow, was a Confederate Army rucksack.

Holton ran over to the bag. "That's gotta be McCarthy's rucksack!" he shouted on his way over.

"Thank God!" Singleton groaned to my right. "I'm already getting sick of rabbit and berries."

"Don't diss it just cause you can't cook worth a damn," Colt teased Singleton, who had reluctantly taken over McCarthy's job as mess cook.

Holton leaned against the tree and reached down to retrieve the ration sack. "Jesus, this thing is heavy!" He strained to pull it from its resting place, but eventually freed it from the water. He placed his arm through the strap and started carrying it back to the gathered crowd.

He had only gotten a few steps when he suddenly squealed and let the bag fall off of him onto the ground.

"What the hell got into your panties?" Olmstead taunted. Zollenger shot him a warning glare and Olmstead resumed his silence.

"What is it, Corporal?" Wilkes asked.

"Something just moved in there, sir." Holton explained, pointing down at the bag.

"Ah, shit!" Zollenger groused. "Some damn critter's probably gotten in there, eating up our rations." He whistled to get Holton's attention and then threw him over his revolver. "Open it up and shoot the son of a bitch when he goes scurrying."

Holton nodded, seeming to gather himself. He, inched forward, careful to keep the pistol's barrel pointed at the bag. As he neared it, I saw something shift under the canvas.

Holton carefully reached down and undid the bag's clasp, throwing the cover open. He stared in the bag momentarily, then his eyes damn near bulged out of his skull as he flailed backwards onto his ass. He fired two shots into the bag and scurried away on all fours.

"Jesus Christ, Corporal!" Zollenger shouted. "Don't shoot the damn bag!" He whistled at the nearest man, Colt, and tossed him his rifle, gesturing for him to keep an eye on Olmstead. He then jogged over to the sack.

"What was it?" Zollenger asked, nearing the bag. "Some rabid squirrel, guessing by the way you about pissed your damn pants." He leaned down to grab the bottom of the sack, making ready to dump out the contents. Whatever was inside was still moving.

Holton emphatically shook his head. "Not no squirrel, Sergeant Major," he cried. "I think...I think it's McCarthy."

The entire troop froze at Holton's words. Zollenger included, who stopped overturning the bag to stare down at it. After a moment, he continued on, letting the bag's contents spill out to the ground.

Or *plop* to the ground would be a better description.

A thick, black glob fell from the bag, landing with a sickening sploosh as it hit dead leaves and dirt. Though, upon further glance, it wasn't entirely a black glob. The paleness of human flesh could be seen mixed in with the blackness. From the bottom of the glob, two legs stuck out, the goo slowly eating its way down the calves. From the side, two arms – mostly only hands and wrists remaining. And, most horrifyingly, from the top, the stump of a neck, McCarthy's head still attached on the other end.

A black stream of viscous fluid ran from his nostrils until it met with another flowing out his mouth and continuing down his cheeks, already pooling in the dirt beneath him. One of his eyes was nothing but a basin of black. Even as we watched, the molten death ate through the surrounding flesh of his eye cavity until the pool was released, sending a flood of muck down his temple.

His other eye, though, that was far worse. Still seemingly whole in his head - other than the thin lines of black running through sclera in place of the usual red – the eyeball rolled towards Zollenger and locked onto him once he was aligned in the pupil's sight.

The sludge in McCarthy's mouth began to bubble. McCarthy was forcing air through its thickness, trying to speak. It wasn't clear, but I'm certain that he was saying, "Help me!"

Standing right next to me, I could hear Singleton fall to his knees and expel a repugnant mix of rabbit and berries into the nearby bush.

"Sergeant Major," Wilkes calmly called out to the stunned Zollenger. "Burn it."

Zollenger immediately scanned the area near his feet. He found a stick lying on the ground and quickly grabbed it up. Singleton tossed him the kerosene canteen. Zollenger caught it, then ripped off the sleeve of his blouse to the elbow. He wrapped the sleeve around the edge of the stick and poured a small stream of the kerosene onto the impromptu torch.

Before he could get the flame going, one long tentacle formed from the midsection of the blob and shot out to wrap around a nearby tree. The long, sleek arm flexed and pulled the remaining mass of the blob up into the high branches. Zollenger instinctively fell backwards as the blob shot past him, eliciting a string of curses, but he somehow managed to keep hold of the unlit torch. However, the canteen fell from his hands. Its acrid contents sloshed from the uncapped neck and soaked into the ground.

The blob was perched upside down, McCarthy's head swinging freely beneath its mass. His jaw was now almost completely eaten away. Other than the dissolving flesh, the blob stayed still up in the tree.

"Sergeant Major, get that torch lit," Wilkes urged.

Zollenger struck the flint towards the torch. It sparked, quickly bursting into fiery life.

No sooner had the torch caught, than another tentacle shot out from the blob, slapping the torch out of Zollenger's hand. The torch flew several yards away, coming to rest in a patch of dirt.

My eyes weren't on the lost torch, however. They stayed glued to Zollenger, who was shouting in intense agony. The tentacle had aimed low while slapping the torch away, careful to avoid its flame.

Instead, it had whipped Zollenger's hand directly, which I saw now was nothing but tattered skin and gore hanging loosely from his wrist.

The blob lowered itself from the tree, a strange rattling sound coming from it as it splat onto the ground. A slit tore along the side of the blob facing Zollenger. The slit widened, revealing a dark eye underneath. Zollenger got his whimpering under control, focusing on the new threat in front of him. The blob was, in turn, focusing on Zollenger.

There was a brief standstill as the two opponents sized each other up. The silence was broken when six tendrils, three on each side of the creature, broke out from the black mass and arced themselves to the ground.

The blob's shift into a grotesque alien spider kicked Zollenger into gear. He winced in what-must-have-been considerable pain as he rose up and scrambled for the burning torch.

The creature didn't hesitate. It immediately shot after Zollenger, chasing him down. The damn thing was fast. Too fast. I realized immediately that Zollenger would never make it to the torch in time.

Silas realized it too. He was nearest the torch and dived for it; scooping it up and tossing it to Zollenger. Zollenger snatched it out of the air and immediately turned with it, bringing it to bear just as the spider blob collapsed on top of him.

As soon as the flaming torch made contact with the glistening flesh; a spark burst and a loud boom cracked through the woods. The creature was fired backwards at an incredible rate, every inch of its body instantly engulfed in flame.

I was reminded me of a fireworks show I had seen a couple years prior. A flare shooting into the air, followed by a loud explosion. The creature admirably mimicked one of those sparkly rockets that had captivated me that day.

"Ha ha! Fuck you!" Zollenger shouted as the beast impacted against a tree, bursting into nothing but a thousand sparks, which then rained down upon the ground. He threw both his arms into the air in celebration. The look of intense pain that crossed his face made plain that he immediately regretted the gesture. He clutched at his bloody stump and collapsed back to the ground. He could still be heard laughing though, even as he writhed in the dirt.

"You alright, Sergeant Major?" Wilkes asked, approaching the downed man with concern etched deep in his face.

"Yes, sir," Zollenger answered, still laughing. "Though I reckon my wife's going to be the one has to jerk my pecker for me from now on." More laughing coupled with wincing.

"We're going to need to get that wrapped up," Wilkes said, not sharing in the humor. "Afraid we can't do much else till we at least get to Richmond."

"Yes, sir," Zollenger replied, his laughter starting to fade.

Colt grabbed some cloth from one of the bags and rushed over to the ailing man. "I'll get this wrapped best that I can, Sergeant Major. Can't promise anything, though. I'm no doctor, just seen them do this a few times out there in the battlefields."

Colt went about wrapping Zollenger's hand, the end result looking as professional as anybody could have asked for, given the circumstances. Zollenger scooted backwards, careful to keep his newly-wrapped stump from dragging on the ground. He stopped with his back against a nearby tree.

"Well, gentleman," Wilkes said, addressing the group in whole, "I think it's safe to say that our worst fears have been proven true. The chaplain, or at least some foul creation of his, appears to still be alive."

"Ah fuck!" Zollenger shouted, interrupting Wilkes' speech. "Where the fuck is Olmstead?"

I looked to where I had last seen Olmstead. He had disappeared at some point during the blob's attack. Heads swiveled as the men started searching for their missing man.

A splash from across the river divulged his fate. We watched as Olmstead climbed from the river to lay out on the opposite bank. Once situated, he stared across the river at his dumbfounded former brothers.

Olmstead threw up both arms, middle fingers extended towards us. "Fuck you, you fucking cunts!" he shouted. "You ain't marching me at gunpoint no more, ya hear!? And I sure as fuck ain't gonna be dissected by no docs in Richmond." Then, for added emphasis, "You all can suck my dick!" He then fell back into the mud laughing.

Zollenger propelled himself around the tree that he had been leaning against, pistol held outstretched in his remaining hand. He fired off two shots, both only managing to kick up the mud near Olmstead's ass.

Olmstead's laughter evaporated as his eyes widened in confusion at the sudden shots from his former captor. He hastily scrambled backwards from the river bank and disappeared into the trees.

"Shit!" Zollenger cursed. "I can't shoot shit with this hand." He let a couple more shots fly into the foliage where Olmstead had vanished.

"Let him go, Sergeant Major," Wilkes ordered. "We've got bigger issues now, wouldn't you say?"

Zollenger turned to his captain and nodded, though I could tell that his current emotions didn't necessarily agree.

"All I know is that I sure as shit ain't getting anywhere near that river," Singleton warned.

"You'll do whatever the hell you're ordered to, soldier!' Zollenger barked, angered at Olmstead's escape.

"No. He's right." Wilkes took a couple steps towards the river, but stopped well short of the muddy bank. "I'm not too keen on the idea of getting into it myself." He crossed his arms around his back and stared silently for a moment, turning his various options over in his mind. Then, without turning, "First Sergeant, is there any kerosene left?"

Colt retrieved the spilt canteen and gave it a small shake. "I'm afraid not, sir. It's completely empty." He confirmed this by holding the canteen upside down. Nothing more than a drop fell from its mouth.

"The sun has nearly left today behind already and we will need time to find a better way of crossing this river," Wilkes thought out loud.

Another prolonged silence followed, after which Wilkes finally turned back to his men. "We know that fire kills whatever these demons are, so let's get one burning, and *keep* it burning. At least until we concoct a suitable plan to leave this abominable place behind.

"Winny," Wilkes pointed over to me, "gather up the oil lamps. I doubt there's much left in them at this point, but we can use whatever remains to get a fire going. First Sergeant, take Private Singleton with you and gather up some firewood. At least, enough to get us through the night.

The two men saluted and ran off to accomplish their given mission.

"And stay together!" Wilkes shouted after them. "I don't want any man out on his own!"

Wilkes turned to Silas. "Sergeant Armington, perhaps you would be kind enough to accompany Corporal Holton and find us something to eat?"

Both men nodded and ran off in the opposite direction of Colt and Singleton.

"What about me, sir?" Zollenger asked from his resumed resting spot against the tree.

"You rest up, Sergeant Major," Wilkes said, his tone laced with sympathy. "I'd say it's been a particularly rough day for you and I'm still going to be in need of your services until our journey's end."

Zollenger sat stiff for a moment, looking like he wanted to argue the point. He soon relented though and leaned back against the tree, pulling his cap brim low over his eyes. "I suppose I could use a nap, though I find that prospect rather unlikely. This fucking nub hurts like a son of a bitch."

I could still hear Zollenger grumbling as I set off to accomplish my task. I silently hoped that the other men would make it back soon. The sky was quickly darkening, the shadows consuming the land.

July 12ᵗʰ, 1863

"Wake up, boy!"

The unmistakable booming voice of the chaplain woke me from my sleep. I was unable to open my eyes at first, left wallowing in the darkness.

"Open your eyes, boy! See what God hath wrought."

I realized that the voice was not falling onto my ear drums, but rather was being spoken directly into my mind. As if that realization somehow acted as a mysterious key to my eyelids, I was suddenly able to open them and behold my strange surroundings.

I was no longer in my tent. I found myself lying out among the trees. The night sky impenetrably dark, but my vision held a strange sort of illumination that kept the blackness from completely overtaking it.

As I focused on my surroundings, I could hear the rush of the river coming from somewhere not too far off. It seemed that it was further than where I had laid myself to rest, but it was still near enough to be readily identifiable.

"Now observe God's power." Lyman's voice again, still heard only with my internal senses.

"Mr. Olmstead," Lyman's voice called out. I still wasn't hearing it with my ears, but I had the sense that I wasn't the only one able to hear these latest words. "Mr. Olmstead, wake up. God beckons."

A rustling broke from a bush near where I was standing. I looked over and saw Olmstead lying there, rubbing the sleep from his eyes. He searched around for what had awaken him, his gaze falling directly on me several times as his head scanned the forest. They never stopped to rest on me, however. I sensed that Olmstead couldn't see me, as if I was nothing more than a phantom stalking the night.

"Mr. Olmstead." Lyman again.

"What the fuck?" Olmstead asked, scanning the trees more frantically now. "Who the fuck is that? Show yourself!"

"You know who it is."

The fear permeating Olmstead's eyes told me that he did indeed recognize the voice.

"Ah, hell no! Fuck you, man," Olmstead cried, shaking his head enough that I was afraid it may just come off. "You stay the fuck away from me, ya hear!"

"Come, Mr. Olmstead. Your God is calling you."

"He's not my god, you son of a bitch!"

Lyman's spectral voice chuckled. "But, Mr. Olmstead, you partook of God's body. He *is* your God now."

Olmstead cowered further into the bush that he had been resting in.

"Stand up, Mr. Olmstead!" Lyman's voice ordered with strong authority.

Olmstead shot to his feet. The strange way he rose, and the confusion affixed in his gaze, led me to believe that the action was not voluntary.

"What the fuck!?" Olmstead squeaked.

"Now," Lyman commanded, "come to me."

Olmstead's left foot shot forward. Then his right. The cycle repeated, carrying Olmstead's body towards the sound of the river in the distance. "Fuck! Fuck! What the fuck is going on!?" Olmstead's voice was trembling.

I followed Olmstead as he shuffled his way to the river. Partly because I was curious, I'll admit, but mostly because I didn't really feel that I had a choice.

We walked for several minutes, finally breaking free of the dense foliage and emerging onto the bank of the winding river. I was surprised to see that we were not at the bank near the campsite. I glanced down the river's length and couldn't spot the turn that had trapped us. I don't know how far we were from the camp, but knew that this spot was likely a good distance further down the river's path.

Olmstead's gaze never turned down the river. Instead, it was frozen staring straight out towards the river's center; or, more precisely, at the figure sitting cross-legged *atop* the flowing water.

The chaplain, Lyman Abernathy.

He was now clothed in gray. Apparently, he had taken McCarthy's uniform whenever he had...umm...well, done whatever he had done to the poor cook.

"Oh God in Heaven," Olmstead cried, motioning the symbol of the cross as he fell to his knees.

"No. Not in Heaven." Lyman smiled.

"What do you want with me?" Olmstead asked, his lip quivering.

"*I* want nothing but to serve God. And God has called for you to serve him as well."

Olmstead's eyes welled up with tears. "Please! Let me go! I'll do anything you want, just let me go!" he begged.

"I assure you, you will do anything *He* wants."

Lyman rose from his cross-legged position and walked across the water towards shore. His steps sunk more into the mud of the shore than they had in the water rushing past. He stopped when he reached Olmstead.

Lyman placed his hand on top of Olmstead's head. "Are you ready to serve your God?"

Olmstead's sobbing paused as he looked up into the eyes of the chaplain. I could see the fires of hatred begin to burn bright within.

"Fuck you and fuck your God!" Olmstead spat onto the chaplain's leg.

If Lyman was offended, he did not show it. The smile stayed pasted to his face as if were made of concrete.

"I seem to remember, not too long ago, you threatening to cut off my phallus and use it to silence the Union sergeant."

Olmstead stayed silent, unsure where this was going.

"Seems a fitting way to silence a blasphemer," Lyman chillingly concluded.

"What?" Olmstead asked, the hate once again being replaced by terror.

The chaplain undid the clasp on his gray trousers, letting them fall around his ankles. His member waved free in the air, looking like a large snake ready to snatch some prey. The veins running through it were black against the severely pale skin.

"Go ahead," he ordered. "Gag yourself."

The tears had once again engulfed Olmstead's eyes as his head inched forward. His mouth wrapped around Lyman's cock, eliciting muffled wails of emotional agony from the man. His head kept inching forward until the long shaft hit the back of his mouth.

Then he kept moving forward.

Olmstead gagged as the chaplain's cock slid down his throat, his neck bulging to indicate its progress through his esophagus. Spittle, soon accompanied by vomit, leaked out of Olmstead's mouth, as he continued to choke Lyman's manhood down.

He finally was able to stop when his lips touched upon Lyman's groin.

"Now, finish the job," Lyman commanded. Obviously unable to speak, Olmstead looked questioningly up into Lyman's face.

"Go ahead," Lyman answered, "bite it off."

With a deluge of tears pouring free, Olmstead bit. His teeth sunk through the chaplain's flesh. Easily at first, but some gnawing was required towards the end.

Not a single ounce of pain registered on Lyman's face. Only the concrete smile.

Once Olmstead had completed the grisly task, a small piece of the member's base remained protruding from his lips, black sludge leaking from its severed base. It started to wiggle, like the ass of rattlesnake. I would have sworn that I had even heard a rattle as it writhed between his lips. It squirmed itself deep down Olmstead's throat, first disappearing between his lips, then the bulge disappearing from his throat.

Olmstead collapsed to the ground and wept, no longer of a sanity to do anything else.

Lyman left Olmstead to bawl on the ground, stepping back into the river. This time he sank into the water, up to his waist. He stood like that for a moment before turning back around, then emerged once again. As the water dripped from his body, I could see that his penis had completely reformed in all of its previous glory.

Lyman pulled up his trousers and secured them before finally turning to me.

"Go, boy. Get your rest," he said. "For in the morning, I will come to collect you into the service of God."

I gulped, never having felt a fear as intense before. His ghoulish grin was the last thing I saw as everything faded to black.

******

My foot shaking again. My ears – my real ears – hearing "Winny. Wake up."

My eyes opened to Silas, shaking me awake. Also, instead of the usual darkness outside, I saw that the sun had already ascended the horizon.

"Oh shit," I whispered. Silas looked at me with confusion.

I, however, was no longer confused. Three realizations hit me as I thrust off my blankets. The first was that the coiling blackness in my tent had not been a dream. Secondly, neither had the horrible scene I had just witnessed.

The third...well, the third was: "It's morning already. He's coming!"

I sprang from my tent, directly past a befuddled Silas.

"Captain!" I shouted, running towards where he was sitting near the fire. "Captain! He's coming!"

"Whoa, Winny. Slow down," Wilkes demanded. "Who's coming?"

"The chaplain, sir," I said, huffing slightly from the run and shock. "He's alive and he's coming here now!'

Wilkes momentarily wrestled with my warning, then threw his mug down and began frantically motioning for the men to gather around.

"What the fuck!?" I heard Zollenger shout. I looked over to where the sergeant major was sitting against a tree and knew that it was already too late.

Marching across the water was Lyman, heading directly towards us. Zollenger reacted quickly. He aimed his pistol and fired off several shots. None managed to slow the chaplain's progress.

As I studied the approaching wraith, I noticed that something seemed different about him. He was incredibly fat. His stomach wasn't just bulging - it was like a large sack hanging down to his knees, flopping with every step he took.

This oddity had no effect on Zollenger, though. He reloaded and kept firing into the man.

When the chaplain reached Zollenger, he didn't even break stride, simply swiping the gun away from him and tossing it towards the river bank. It landed in the muck with a loud splat.

The rest of the men scrambled for their weapons, retrieving them and firing away. Every bullet wound would close almost as soon as it was inflicted. The only response Lyman gave to the gunfire was towards Singleton, who had retrieved his shotgun. Lyman's tongue – or, more accurately, a long black tendril that had taken the place of

Lyman's tongue – darted several yards out of his mouth and coiled around the shotgun. The tongue wrestled the gun from Singleton's grip and launched it towards the river. It, too, landed in the mud, clanking against Zollenger's pistol.

The chaplain sucked the tongue back into his mouth and kept walking.

Lyman came to a stop in front of the campfire and stared at it thoughtfully. The men stopped firing, watching the strange man's actions with suspense.

Wilkes must have been the first to realize what was about to happen. He broke from the trance, firing his rifle and screaming "No!"

Lyman's mouth opened, the gaping hole growing much larger than any normal human mouth could possibly stretch. Suddenly, a deluge of river water forced its way out of his mouth and onto the fire. Lyman's stomach shrunk down with ever gallon expelled, until it had resumed its normal shape.

By that time, the fire had been completely doused.

"Now, with that taken care of..." Lyman didn't finish the sentence, just rubbed his hands together as if he were wiping them clean.

Zollenger eyed the shotgun. He burst from his perch and sprinted towards it. He had nearly reached it when something sleek and black rocketed from the river and collided into him. A ball of black and Zollenger rolled along the ground for a moment, stopping with the black shape atop of the sergeant major.

I could tell right away that I was looking at what had become of Olmstead, though it barely looked human at all. A humanoid form, to be sure; with two legs, two arms, and a head, but the entire body was black. His back was ridged, glimmering with glossy scales. The fingers and toes were webbed with a black film connecting them together on each appendage. His ears had grown large and his eyes bulged outward. The pupils they contained stretched vertically, appearing reptilian in nature.

Movement at his neck caught my eye. I watched as three slits palpitated on each side. Gills were the closest thing I could relate them too.

Olmstead had grown large and muscular in his transformation. And, of course, completely black. The strength from his new musculature was made apparent when he stood and brought Zollenger up with him, effortlessly holding the large man off of the ground at arm's length.

Zollenger struggled, powerless in Olmstead's grip. Olmstead stared at him with his reptilian eyes. Zollenger stared back in terror, watching as Olmstead's eyes blinked from both the top and the sides.

I swear I saw a smile creep across Olmstead's lips before his tongue whipped out, lodging itself deep into Zollenger's throat. Zollenger continued struggling, now also choking. We all watched helplessly as three fat bulbs traveled through the inside of Olmstead's tongue, depositing their contents somewhere inside Zollenger.

Once complete, Olmstead casually dropped Zollenger and turned towards the other members of the camp.

I broke from my stance and turned to run, intending to lose myself in the trees.

"Stop, boy!" Lyman barked. "Witness God's hand at work!" His order halted me before I had even made it two steps into my escape. The prior night's incident with Olmstead weighed heavy on my mind as my body refused to obey my own command.

Colt' rifle cracked loudly as Olmstead next fixated on him. Colt' bullets clearly impacted Olmstead's body, but seemed to disappear inside his muscled, tarry body. Several other rifles were firing as well; Wilkes and Singleton having joined in on the salvo.

A quick glance to the chaplain revealed that he sat cross-legged, letting the events play out before him. His seemed to just be enjoying the show, as if it were no more than an amusing act at a traveling circus.

Olmstead continued forward, undaunted by the irrelevant pricks of the bullets. Colt kept firing, frantically hoping that one would eventually bring the beast down. Finally, Colt' rifle clicked on empty. He hastily tried to reload it, but Olmstead was on him before he could snap home the final round.

Olmstead squeezed his large, webbed hands around Colt' shoulders, lifting him off the ground much like he had Zollenger. Unlike with Zollenger, however, the sizzling started as soon as the large appendages gripped Colt' flesh.

"He can control it," I blurted. Silas looked over at me, having heard my words. Understanding dawned on him as he too noticed the hands now absorbing the skin from Colt' shoulders.

Colt was howling in agony as the monster held him high. His weeping eyes grew large as a webbed series of black spikes emerged from out of the slime that topped Olmstead's head. The spikes ran back from his creased forehead to the rear of what-had-been Olmstead's hairline. Of course, all hair had disappeared off the man, leaving only the shiny black muck.

The spikes gleamed in the light. They weren't large, but they appeared menacing, nonetheless. The Olmstead creature let loose a loud, thumping victory shout towards the sky, the pitch containing entirely too much bass for human vocal chords to achieve.

Olmstead thrust his head forward, impaling the spikes straight through Colt' abdomen. Colt' wails raised several octaves as Olmstead twisted his head, forcing it further into Colt' body. Soon the spikes emerged from his spine, followed by the rest of Olmstead's head. Olmstead kept pushing through until Colt was completely ripped in half, Olmstead now covered in red and white bits of Colt' innards.

Olmstead flung both halves of Colt in opposite directions. The upper half crashed against a tree and crumpled to the ground. A black stain was already starting to eat away at his torso.

Somehow, Colt was still screaming.

"Fuck!" Silas shouted next to me.

Olmstead howled in triumph again, then caught sight of Holton. His feet resumed loudly stomping, now in Holton's direction. Holton, still several yards away from the monster, quickly turned and fled. He obviously held no interest in taking a stand and firing into the beast as Colt had.

"We're all going to die if we can't get a flame going," Silas whispered to me, watching the creature give chase to Holton.

"You have a flint on you?" I asked. My body was frozen, but not my mind. "Maybe just a spark would be enough. These things seem pretty volatile."

Silas considered it. "Maybe," he reluctantly agreed, "but I'm not going to just stroll up to him and find out that it's not."

Holton arrived at a tall tree and began scrambling up it. Olmstead continued stomping towards him.

"We need something better." Silas scanned around for anything that could help. His eyes lit on his rifle and a small grin crept onto his lips. "Maybe," he whispered, more to himself than to me. Silas turned back towards the nearest tent and ran behind it. I saw him scoop up one of the serving bowls before disappearing.

More shots rang out and I turned back to Holton. He was perched on a thick tree branch, high off the ground. Having reached a relative place of safety, he began firing into the pursuing creature. Holton was carefully aiming for Olmstead's head, hoping a head shot would do the trick.

It didn't.

Olmstead arrived at the tree and stopped, snarling up at Holton.

"Fuck you, you son of a bitch!" Holton yelled, reloading his rifle and firing off another volley into the creature.

Olmstead slapped one hand onto the tree. A loud sucking sound could be heard as his finned phalanges made contact. He followed with the other hand, higher up the tree than the first. The original hand released, then connected even higher. Olmstead was using some kind of suction in his palms to scale the tree.

Holton's eyes widened to damn near splitting. He started firing his weapon at Olmstead much more urgently than before. Olmstead kept climbing.

"Captain!' Zollenger's voice rang out from where he lay out near the river bank.

Wilkes, who was digging through an ammunition satchel, looked up at the voice.

"Captain, they're in me! I can feel them," Zollenger whimpered.

Zollenger's belly had swollen large. Three lumps could be seen moving around just under the skin.

Wilkes studied this for a moment, then continued filling his pockets with rounds. When done, he rushed over near the sergeant major's side, kneeling next to him.

"Stay back!" Holton's cries drew my attention back to the tree. Olmstead had arrived at the branch where Holton was perched. A couple more rifle blasts into the fish-like man, and Olmstead started out along the limb.

Holton crawled backward, but was quickly running out of branch. The wood started to groan under Holton's weight. With every further scoot, the limb groaned louder.

Until, finally, it *snapped*.

Holton began falling with the branch out into the open air. Olmstead, who had closed the distance, shot out his paw and seized Holton's throat, instantly halting his descent. Holton's legs flailed in a frenzy as he was slowly lifted back to Olmstead's eye level. The sizzling had started at Holton's throat, though the high-pitched wails he elicited were less yelps of pain than screams of terror.

Olmstead's puffy, amphibian-like lips briefly curled into a smirk as he held Holton aloft, before spreading wide. Then wider. Then even wider! Until finally Olmstead's mouth opened far wider than any orifice its size had any right. Olmstead's lips formed a freakish oblong angle as they thrust forward, engulfing Holton's upper body down past his pectorals. The monster swung its head upwards, Holton's legs now kicking towards the sky. Olmstead's lips stretched couple inches further down Holton's body, pulling him further down his gullet. The whole scene reminiscent of a snake swallowing the family cat.

"Oh God!" Wilkes shouted, though not at the grisly scene in the tree. Looking over, I saw that he was standing over Zollenger, watching his pulsating stomach.

A wide gorge had split open the sergeant major's stomach. The laceration grew longer as something hit against the inside of Zollenger's abdomen, an inch or so at a time. Spouts of red and black mist would erupt each time the gash lengthened. Soon, a shining, round clump of black appeared in the split. Slowly, the round bulb raised up revealing a hideous face. My stomach clenched as the small black head peeked out into its brand new world. A high-pitched shrill escaped the baby creature's lungs as it launched itself from Zollenger's midsection. It was soon joined by two others, who picked themselves up from where they had landed and started surveying their new surroundings.

Wilkes wasted no time. He pointed his pistol at the first creature and fired into it. The impact threw the tiny creature back several feet. It quickly situated itself upon landing in the dirt. The infant monster found Wilkes with scorn in its features and hissed loudly towards its attacker. Wilkes fired again, missing this time. The creature hissed again before turning to scurry off into the woods. It was soon followed by its two brothers.

Wilkes seemed determined to not let them get away. He began giving chase, firing more rounds at the escaping brood. He hadn't gone far when something large came out of nowhere, crashing into him and knocking him to the ground. There he stayed, lackadaisical groans of pain the only indication he was still alive.

The object that had crashed into him finally rolled to a stop. It was a hefty branch from one of the surrounding trees. It didn't take long to realize that it had been thrown by Olmstead. The Olmstead creature was still perched high on the tree. His lips were now curled around Holton's knees, continuing to him further down.

Olmstead was staring hatefully at the attacker of his progeny, a hate-filled hissing sound working its way around the large mound of flesh in his throat. Wilkes clumsily rolled onto his back, not noticing the creature's hateful stare. Not noticing much of anything, by the looks of it. The impact had left him completely dazed.

Olmstead leaped down from the tree branch, landing on his feet with a heavy thud. His lips, now surrounding Holton's calves, stretched out until they curled around the heels of the soldier's boots. He pulled him the rest of the way down his gullet, his meal now completely engulfed. Throughout it all, his hateful eyes never left Wilkes' disoriented form.

"Captain Wilkes!" I shouted. "Get up! He's coming for you!" Wilkes gave no indication that he had heard me.

Olmstead reared back like a bull ready to strike, then thrust himself forward, galloping towards the captain.

Suddenly, a thunderous roar split the air. Olmstead's advance was halted midstride, causing the broad beast to skid along the ground, askew from his objective.

I looked towards the loud explosion. It was Singleton, having reclaimed his shotgun from the bank's muck. He must have made his way around to it through the trees, out of the sight of Olmstead and the chaplain.

Singleton fired off the other barrel. The monster bucked at the impact, but showed no sign of injury. While Singleton reloaded, Olmstead shifted glances between Wilkes and Singleton. Deciding that Wilkes wasn't going to be making a fleeting escape anytime soon, Olmstead chose Singleton.

Seeing Olmstead's approach, Singleton sprinted off towards the trees, still fumbling to get the rounds in their respective chambers. Olmstead followed until they both vanished into the foliage.

"Singleton!" Silas yelled, emerging from behind the tent. He was carrying the bowl, some kind of powdery substance loosely shifting around the bottom. "I need that fucker here! Bring him back to camp!"

Two ringing blasts were the only answer he received.

"Fuck!" Silas cursed.

It was then that Silas noticed Lyman, still sitting placidly near the remnants of the campfire. "You're next!" Silas promised.

The chaplain smiled. "We shall see, speck."

"What are you doing, Silas?" I asked.

"I'm going to barbeque the chaplain's abomination. *That*'s what I'm going to do." Silas kept his eyes glued on the chaplain, as if daring him to try something.

The chaplain remained placidly sitting. "Do whatever you feel you need to do, Sergeant. I am currently bound by oath from stopping you."

Two more blasts rang out from deep in the woods. Seeing as how he had some time still, Silas prodded further. "What oath?"

"The oath I gave to your President Lincoln that none of his precious Union boys would be affected by God's gifts."

Silas stood too stunned to reply.

"Why do you think your army was able to defeat the forces at Gettysburg?" Lyman continued. "Thus far, your army hasn't been doing so well in this war. Why now would the tide start to turn?

"The answer is that I struck a deal with your dear President. The air at Gettysburg was laced with small particles of God's body. Particles from that bottle the Confederates found on me. Enough to permeate the air and infect every rebel that breathed it in. Once inside, I was able to control them. Weaken them. Let you Union boys take them."

"Bullshit!" Silas scoffed. Then, considering it, "What do you get in return?"

"Me? Nothing," Lyman dismissed. "God, however, gets to live inside them. Every part of them - every last cell – contains the God's hunger. When those cells die out, God will feast on the nourishment that they provide. It sustains him in his millennial slumber. The process is the same as what you have witnessed here – the consuming of the flesh - only in an infinitely slower manner. They may die earlier than originally fated, but not early enough to raise question."

"Why not just kill them all now?"

"It is not yet time for the whole world's eyes to be opened to God's power," the chaplain answered.

I didn't know what to make of the chaplain's dire tale. I could tell, neither did Silas.

Instead of questioning further, though, Silas turned back to the woods. "Singleton!' he yelled out again.

"Beware though, my oath will not stop God's emissary from defending itself if it's being attacked. Choose your actions wisely," the chaplain warned.

"Silas, what are you planning?" I asked nervously.

"Gunpowder," he answered, swirling the contents of the bowl. "It's not much, just what I was able to get from the rounds in my rifle. It'll be enough, though."

"Enough for what?"

"I *know* this shit will go up with just a spark. I cover him in this, spark it, and end this fucker."

I thought it through and quickly found a vital flaw in his plan. "But, you'll have to be right next to Olmstead to spark it."

Silas' eyes betrayed sorrow as he turned to let them linger on me. "I know," he said, resigned. He let his eyes shift over to the chaplain; the scarred man's warning weighing heavy on his mind.

Silas tore his gaze away from Lyman and let it settle back on me. "Now, get the hell out of here. No matter what happens, just keep running!"

"I can't," I answered, a tear breaking loose from my eye. "He won't let me." I motioned towards the chaplain.

He started asking me what I meant, when he was cut off by two more blasts erupting from the woods. They sounded like they were getting nearer to the camp.

"Thank God! He's still alive," Silas rejoiced, turning towards the fading thunder. "Singleton!" Silas called out again. "Run back to camp! Run back now!"

A loud rustling came from the trees, heading in our direction. I wasn't sure if Singleton had heard Silas or not, but he was nearing the camp either way.

"Sergeant!" Silas and I both flinched at Wilkes' call. He was limping over to us, clutching his side. His face cringed with every awkward step.

"Captain?"

"Give me the bowl." Wilkes gestured towards himself. "This cocksucker's mine!"

If I hadn't been so frozen in terror, I may have laughed at the irony of his statement.

"Pardon me, Captain, but I've got this one." Silas argued.

"The fuck you do! He's slaughtered my men. Damn near all of them!" Wilkes countered. "Now hand over the fucking bowl! I'm not asking, Sergeant."

Silas reluctantly handed the bowl to Wilkes. "You sure you're up for this?" he asked, motioning at Wilkes hobbled form.

Wilkes snatched the dish from him. "You're goddamn right I do." The captain wore a look of determination like I had never seen in a man. "A couple cracked ribs aren't going to stop me from making this son of a bitch pay."

Singleton appeared through the trees, furiously sprinting back into the camp. "He's right behind me!" Singleton screamed when he saw us.

Olmstead soon galloped into view, right on Singleton's tail. Singleton was fast, but Olmstead was faster. In an open clearing now, Olmstead was able to propel himself impossibly high into the air, falling to collide with Singleton's back. Both men collapsed to the ground and rolled in a blur of black and white limbs.

Wilkes immediately took off, hobbling in the direction of the tumbling duo. He still cringed with every step, but his determination propelled him through the pain that he must have been feeling.

The rolling stopped, Olmstead having gained the coveted upper position. The bulky beast grabbed onto Singleton and muscled him onto his back. Singleton could do nothing but scream as Olmstead's tongue slowly snaked out of his dark maw.

Seeing how Singleton's flesh wasn't sizzling, I knew what Olmstead had planned for him. Impregnation, same as Zollenger.

Olmstead's tongue danced in the air, slowly squirming its way forward. Just as it curled back, ready to strike, the metal bowl crashed against the creature's back; a salt and pepper stain left on the beast in the bowl's wake.

Olmstead immediately sucked up his tongue and turned to meet this new threat. Fortunately, Wilkes had already lunged, clinging to Olmstead's back before he could get turned around.

Wilkes had one arm around squeezed around Olmstead's throat to hold himself in place. With his other, he reached into his pocket and pulled out the flint and steel. He gripped the steel piece with his teeth just as Olmstead's defenses kicked in and the sizzling started. Wilkes let loose a muffled howl, but somehow managed to keep his teeth clamped around the steel.

His arm and the entire left side of his body started melting into the creature's hide. The agony must have been gargantuan, but Wilkes kept on task. Using his free hand, he struck the flint. A spark flew, but fizzled out almost immediately. It was too far from the gunpowder stain to ignite it. Wilkes struck it again with the same result.

"It's not going to work," I cried.

Wilkes realized this too and did the only thing he could do. He placed his face right up against Olmstead's back. The sizzling started immediately.

More muffled screaming. The pressure of Wilkes bite on the steel must have been intense as he used it like a doctor did a stick during field surgery.

His hand, shaking now, came up and struck the flint again. Not hard enough as no spark flared.

The left side of Wilkes' skull was already exposed and being eaten away. It wasn't long until even that was eaten away.

The agony was quickly overcoming Wiles' resolve. I could see it in his eyes before his left eyeball made contact with the creature's skin, bursting like a grape as soon as the muck ate through the gelatinous orb's outer wall.

His cheek having already disintegrated, the steel clasped in his teeth now was touching the creature's back. Wilkes dug deep, calling on whatever reserve of will he had left, to strike the flint one last time.

It sparked.

As did the gunpowder stain.

The powder flashed, a billowy white cloud escaping into the air. Less than a second later, a flaming torch erupted on Olmstead's back, quickly consuming the entirety of his oily flesh.

The remaining half of Wilkes' body dropped free from Olmstead's back. It crumpled to the ground and lay still.

"Come on. Let's get the fuck out of here!" Silas exclaimed, using the burning monster as a distraction for the chaplain.

"I told you, I can't..." I was cut off by Silas lifting me on his shoulder. He carried me off towards the trees, running as fast as he could.

Our escape was cut off when the three baby creatures jumped down into our path. Only they weren't exactly babies anymore. Somehow, within the few minutes since they had burst from Zollenger's body, they had grown to half the size of Olmstead. Large enough to keep Silas from trying to bull through them.

"Fuck!" Silas screamed in irritation. He turned back to the chaplain. "I thought you said your monsters wouldn't hurt us unless we attacked them."

"I said they wouldn't hurt *you*. I said nothing of the boy." Lyman glared at me, sending a chill down my spine. "Though, fear not, good Sergeant. I have no plans for him to die today." He took a purely theatrical whiff of the air. "God smells greatness in his blood."

Silas scanned the area, looking for any possible route of escape, but the three creatures had spread out and had us surrounded. His shoulders sagging in defeat, Silas lowered my feet back to the ground.

"If you harm him, I'm going to tell everybody what happened here today," Silas warned. "I don't give a fuck what kind of deal you made – or with who! The army will come bearing down on you and destroy you *and* your demons. You are all tough as shit – I'll give you that – but there are a lot more of us. Your God will fail."

Lyman laughed, though the shrill sound contained no humor. "You think these pitiful drones here represent the extent of God's power? He has innumerable servants all over this universe. On many different planets. In his realm alone, there are more than you could ever count in a lifetime."

"I don't give a fuck about other worlds or realms," Silas challenged. "Only my own. And here, it seems that a shotgun to your head worked well enough. I'll just make sure to keep you close and keep putting rounds into you when you try to reform."

The sinister laugh again. "Yes. That was unfortunate. It would have taken me many weeks to recover from that; except you all made a vital mistake."

Silas stayed silent, inviting the chaplain to clarify.

"You placed me into the water." Lyman said this as if it was a common fact that we should have known. "God thrives in the water. His entire realm is one large sea – more massive than if you placed all of your oceans together. The only break in the sea is one solitary island, floating alone in the middle of its vastness."

"Fantasy!" Silas accused. "There is no such place, you delusional fuck!"

"One day God will awaken and you will hold no qualms of this being fantasy. He will leave his realm and come to plunder yours, through doorways buried deep beneath your oceans. When he arrives, mankind will look upon him and their hope will be completely drained before even the first is consumed."

Lyman leaned down, placing his face only inches from mine. I could smell the rot on his breath as he whispered to me. "Do you want to see it? God's realm?"

I so badly wanted to shake my head, not so much to say "No" as to say "*Fuck* no!" but my body still not being mine, my chin dipped in defiance of my desires. The nod had barely been carried out when the chaplain's black tongue crawled from his mouth. It split at its tip, coming apart like the forked tongue of a reptile. Each end independently waved in the air for a moment, then darted up my nostrils. His tongue tips broke through to my brain and caressed it. The pain immediate, but blessedly brief.

The world faded, and then disappeared altogether.

******

When my eyes opened again, I saw that I was in an unfamiliar place. Darkness surrounded me, deep as the apex of night. The only light came from far on the horizon, both to the left and right of me, as if two suns were dipping away in opposite directions. Two moons were directly overhead, but their dim yellow light did little to illuminate this strange place.

I could hear the sound of rolling thunder, but no cracks of lightning came. The sky was too dark to make out if there were storm clouds overhead.

Upon a second glance towards the moons, I noticed something strange about them. I took a step forward, intending to get a better look, when a small splash arose from my footstep. I looked down, the twilight barely allowing me to make out a ripple as it traveled outward from where my shoe had planted. The ripple traveled equally in all directions, outwards as well as passing underneath me. It was then that I realized I was standing in – no, *on* - water; a large body of it extending as far as my eye could see.

Panic consumed me instantly. I fell backwards, a large splash swallowing me, drenching me in its cold embrace. I thrashed around, frothing the water madly. My body did not sink, but my flailing limbs easily stretched underneath me, submerging in their frenzy. Even at their greatest reach into the depths, no part of me brushed land and I had the feeling – no; somehow I knew with a certainty – that I could extend my limbs for many miles further down and still not touch upon the sea's bottom.

I knew that I was afloat on the great sea that the Chaplain had spoken of. The endless sea.

At the time, given my life-long aquaphobia, I could think of no greater nightmare to have awoken to.

I'm not sure how long my attack of anxiety lasted, but it eventually faded and control of myself was finally restored. I stopped thrashing and took a deep, calming breath. I rose to my feet, amazed that I was standing atop the water and not sinking beneath.

An image of the chaplain walking across the river's surface flared to life in my mind and I shivered.

My anxiety back under control, I turned my head, surveying this strange new world. I found that the gloss of the sea was unbroken in most every direction. All except one. In *that* direction, a giant shape rose from the waters.

An island. Assuredly the one Lyman had spoken of.

It appeared as a mountain rising from the flatness of the water, hovering just within the spillage of light from the retreating suns. Near its edge, I could see many buildings, reminiscent of Spanish design with their earthy tones. Small houses, mostly; though some larger buildings could be seen mixed in with the others. It was hard to be sure of their exact nature, as their upper sections were obscured by a thick fog that circled the lower levels of the isle.

As my eyes traveled up the mountain's length, they registered movement; lots of it. It was as if the island itself were writhing. My eyes focused in on the activity and I realized that it wasn't the island writhing, but rather millions of the amphibian-like creatures occupying its surface. Some were the jet black of Olmstead and his brood; but far more were of a greenish hue. The entire upper half of the island swarmed with their activity.

At the island's apex, two similar creatures sat atop marble thrones; only these creatures were enormous. They easily outsized the others tenfold. One looked feminine, the other masculine. I took them as some kind of king and queen of this realm.

I soon realized that the rolling thunder I had heard was coming from the island; only it wasn't thunder at all. It was the millions of amphibian-creatures chanting, though I couldn't make out what they were saying. I heard the syllable well enough, but they made no sense to me. Some sort of language that I had never before heard. Their arms were raised in some sort of worshipping ceremony for the king and queen.

Were one of these royals the God the chaplain served?

Seeing the worshippers made me think so, at first; but something was wrong with the scene. The worshippers' arms were pointed in the wrong direction. The millions weren't pointing up at the royals at all, but towards the skyline above me.

I turned to see if I had missed something behind me, but there was nothing but the impenetrable darkness.

Then I remembered the two moons. The strange way they had twitched upon my second inspection before I had lost my wits upon notice of the great sea. I brought my gaze up to where they hung in the sky and I gasped. I now had no trouble at seeing what they really were. Not moons at all.

They were eyes!

Colossal yellow discs that hung high above me. They burned like fire, but in their center was a spot of darkness. Realizing what these moons actually were, my mind easily interpreted the rest of the scenery around me.

The sky was still dark, but it wasn't night that had fallen on this world. It was a gigantic entity, larger than anything I had ever known - larger than anything I could have even imagined. So monumental was the behemoth, it was blotting out the light of the sun. What I had mistaken for two receding suns at the horizon was the light of only one sun, appearing at the edges of this being's gargantuan body. Two enormous wings stretched out from its back; so large only their roots were in view, the rest lost somewhere over the horizon.

Its face seemed to be moving in an unnatural way. The lack of light, coupled with the giant's black skin, made the source of the movement hard to make out. My first thought was of the coiling snakes that had formed in the top of my tent.

And this colossus was hovering over me - its fiery gaze boring into my soul.

An intense terror overtook me; so great was it that I could feel it ripping at my skin, roiling in my gut. Even the intense pain of my heart bursting in my chest barely went noticed above its intensity. My temples throbbed so mightily they split open from the pressure. Hives grew to cover my skin, growing so massive they, themselves, burst open. Shards of bone, which had since shattered from the intense shaking of my body, toppled out from the fresh lacerations where the hives had stood.

Then I was no longer standing atop the water. My body plunged through the surface, sinking downwards into its cold depths.

I no longer feared the water, though. Something *far* more terrifying had taken its place.

I continued sinking until the last vestiges of light had vanished, replaced with the eternal darkness of the depths.

******

My eyes shot open again; this time to the scarred, grotesque sneer of the chaplain.

"Welcome back, boy!" he greeted.

"You okay, Winny?" Silas asked, breaking free from the grasp of one of the amphibian men. He knelt next to me and helped me up from where I had fallen during my dreamlike vision.

My mind was muddled, but I was cognizant enough to know that I was rambling on and on about deep water, islands...and especially of behemoths. Silas kept questioning me during my rambles and I struggled mightily to gain control of my wits. When finally in control enough to speak coherently, I recited all that the vision had revealed to me.

Judging by Silas' baffled expression, coherency hadn't cleared up the issue.

"What was that place?" I asked the chaplain. "What was that monstrous being that blocked the sun?" As I asked these questions, I noticed that there was a banging in my head. A rhythmic beat of something that had followed me out of that nightmare world. "And what were those millions of frog creatures chanting? I can still hear them in my head, warbling on and on."

"Ah, yes…" Lyman's lips curled into a nefarious grin. "The song of God," he answered. "The frog people, as you call them, are the minions of God, known as the Deep Ones. The song: 'Ph'nglui mglw'nafh Cthulhu R'lyeh wgah'nagl fhtagn'." Lyman's body shook as he recited the chant, his eyes rolling upwards as if the guttural words were bringing him to orgasm. Then, his eyes back on me and his smile so wide I feared his cheeks were going to split apart, he translated.

"In his house at R'lyeh, dead Cthulhu waits dreaming."

Lyman gave us a moment to reflect on the words before continuing.

"The great being that you witnessed was indeed God. The great god Cthulhu. The place, R'lyeh; God's realm where he slumbers. It is connected to all the worlds – all the dark corners of the universe – through passages buried deep in the seas.

"The island is named Y'ha-nlthlei. Sitting atop it were Mother Hydra and Father Dagon; God's most trusted servants and rulers of the Deep Ones. The Deep Ones themselves serve many purposes, depending on their calling. For instance, the Confederate Olmstead was chosen as a Phalli; or, an impregnator, to be crude."

"I always knew that guy was a dick," Silas mumbled behind me. His attempt at humor was lost on me, however. My stomach turned at the memory of how Olmstead had been "converted" to his calling.

"What of the squirming shadows on his face?" I asked, feeling a dire need to understand what I had witnessed.

"That *was* his face. Or more accurately, those were many tendrils which act as his mouth, nose, and ears; shaped to you like the tentacles of an octopus, but far more powerful than that of the measly cephalopod. A mere scraping from one was placed in the bottle that I had carried with me into Gettysburg."

A curious gleam entered the chaplain's eye as he studied me.

"Now you, boy...I'm not sure what great calling God has chosen you for. The word 'prophet' keeps ringing in my head when I inhale the sweet scent of your blood. I must admit, that is a new one to me."

I forced a wad of spittle down my throat as I fearfully contemplated the connotations of his statement.

"I look forward to seeing what form *you* will take."

Lyman slowly brought his hand up to hover in front of my face. He extended his index finger and brought it forward until it gently rested on my lips.

Then he pushed it through them. Deep enough that I nearly gagged on it.

"You've seen a ritual quite similar to this play out before, haven't you?" It was a tease from him. One I couldn't answer with his digit jammed against my uvula. "Meaning that you already know what to do."

I tried pulling away - I even tried shaking my head free - but my body was locked tight by the chaplain's control. The only response I was able to manage were the tears welling in my eyes.

"Now," the chaplain paused, smirking. "Bite!"

And I did. I didn't want to. I tried to not – oh Lord, I did I try – but my teeth bit into his flesh anyway, a salty-sweet taste like fish oil erupting into my mouth as my teeth gnawed through his skin.

My body pushed through my revulsion to continue grinding my teeth. They kept gnashing away at the chaplain's finger until it finally detached from the rest of him. As Lyman pulled his hand away, I could feel the wormlike figure squirming against my tongue.

I knew what was coming next. He'd order me to swallow the vile thing. Then it'd be over. *I'd* be over. I'd morph into whatever hideous creature his God desired for me, and that would be that.

I tried everything in my power to spit it out before the words could leave his mouth, but to no avail. I even tried willing myself to vomit, but even that normally autonomous function was completely out of my control.

"Now, boy…" Here it came. "Sw…"

I more felt than heard the shotgun blast as Lyman's head disintegrated into nothing but mist in front of me.

"Ha ha! Fuck you, Father, for you have sinned!" It was Singleton, hooting in triumph, the shotgun's barrel still smoking in his hand. Given all that had happened, I hadn't even noticed that he had managed to escape as Wilkes had pounced onto Olmstead's back.

Self-control over my body rushed through me and I hurriedly spit out the still-writhing finger inside my mouth. It fell to the ground – completely black now – and I stomped it into the dirt.

No sooner had I raised my foot than the three Deep Ones rushed past me and dove atop Singleton. The soldier disappeared in a furious frenzy of black flesh as the creatures unrelentingly tore into him. A geyser of blood and offal the only indication that a human being had been in that flailing mass of limbs.

"Singleton," I called out. I took a step in his direction, as if there was something I could do anything to help the man. Silas' hand fell on my shoulder, stopping me.

"Winny! We have to go! Before they turn back to us!"

He was right. I'm not sure if the beasts would have attacked us in that field – not knowing if the chaplain's oath still applied - but now that I controlled my own body again, I wasn't sticking around to find out.

I silently said a silent goodbye to the men who had lost their lives in that accursed place, then turned to join Silas.

We ran and we ran…

…never looking back.

March 22ⁿᵈ, 1884

It only took two days for us to return to Gettysburg – such was our haste – but over twenty years before the nightmares of those preceding days finally stopped plaguing me.

For a while, at least.

I was now many years into my adulthood, but I had not enjoyed a normal life. Many thought me peculiar. Most would agree that I was an introvert by nature.

I had never been married, and had only ever once attempted a romantic relationship of any kind. Only one evening out together – more a comedy of errors than an actual courtship - and that experiment came quickly to an end.

It wasn't that I had an avulsion to society. The desire was there, but the nightmares provided me little sleep. A cloud of dread and paranoia constantly hovered over me. I was wholly unable to be good company.

I took up a job as a traveling salesman, much like my father before me. I found it comforting to visit new places. To be able to lose myself in towns that had no idea who I was, or what reputation I carried with me. Places where there were no wicked rumors about me, as tended to happen when I stayed in any one place for too long.

On this particular date in March, I was contacted by a man who claimed to be from some university in Massachusetts that I had never before heard of. Some institution named Miskatonic University. In later years, I would attempt to locate this university, but to no avail. It was as if the place had never actually existed.

This man related that he held a book that he wished to grant to me. When prompted, he refused to reveal a reason why. Only offering a vague explanation of sorts.

"I can hear it calling for you."

Curious, I let the man into my suite for more information. I was surprised that he had it on him, wrapped in a rag dotted with stains that held the vague appearance of blood; though, if so, many years had passed since the rag had collected it.

The man walked to a low, wooden table that I had stashed in a corner. He placed the stained bundle gently on the table and stepped away from it, not bothering to unwrap the book within.

"I leave this book for your perusal. It holds a great power, so be careful not to lose yourself in it." He turned, as if he had already satisfactorily answered any concerns a man would have to such a mysterious offering.

"Wait," I tried, as he stepped to my door.

"I am afraid I cannot, sir. I must not be near when you open the book."

"For God's sake, man," I blurted, though the deistical title was not a word I used often anymore. "At least tell me the name of the book before you go!"

He stopped, one foot already out the door, and considered my request. "It is called the Necronomicon," he finally answered. "Now, good day to you, sir." He closed the door behind him, disappearing from my sight for eternity.

I stared at the wrapped bundle for many minutes before I dared approach it. When I finally did, it was almost like my feet floated in the air, carrying me to it.

I unfolded the splotched cloth from over the book. Inside was a leather tome of quite some age. Only, the dried leather held a different hue than what you would find from a normal bovine hide. It appeared eerily like the dried skin of a human. The flesh was stretched over the pages and bound together by several rough hems that ran haphazardly throughout the cover.

A quiet voice within was telling me that I should be feeling horrified as I stared at the macabre canvas, but I couldn't shake a queer sort of jubilation. Both my mind and heart were screaming at me to open the manual and behold its secrets. I gripped the edge of the cover and something stayed my hand. I couldn't say what, but when my fingers made contact with the leathery flesh, they froze.

I wanted this too badly! How could it be so? I had never heard of this book before. Why should I so eagerly want to peer into it? Especially when, underneath the titillation, I could feel a darkness emanating from the worn pages.

Something felt wrong…horribly wrong.

I snatched my hand away from the book, as if it were a hot coal fresh from the fire. I rewrapped the dingy cloth around it and immediately carried it out of my room.

Luckily, I was just outside of the city of New York, where I knew a man who collected antiquities; most notably rare books. His name was Joseph Curwen and we had twice met on my various travels and he had treated me with friendliness and humor.

I hopped on the nearest train and rode it into the bustling metropolis. I met up with him at a favorite bar that he had introduced me to and I passed him the bundled tome. When I told him of the rag's contents, his eyes lit with great esteem, but I could also tell that he held the book with cautious regard. He revealed to me many stories about this work that had been passed down through the ages.

The more I heard of it, the happier I was that I had stopped myself from browsing through its pages.

After several hours of drunken parlay, we left our own separate ways. Joseph took the book and departed with the dreadful thing clutched under his arm.

The nightmares that had plagued me for so long, departed with it.

June 14ᵗʰ, 1889

Years had passed since I had passed the Necronomicon off to Joseph Curwen. All of my fears having fled, I had managed to make a normal life for myself.

I had finally stopped running – which is what I realized that I had been doing all of those years as a salesman – and had settled down in Rochester, New York. I had even gotten gainful employment as a blacksmith.

I had made friends with many of the locals and had even hosted parties at my place. Real parties! Something I never would have thought possible during my years of seclusion.

To lay eyes on me the morning of that date, you'd see that I was dressed in my best. For this was my wedding day…the day I married your mother.

Such a beautiful woman Sarah was when I had met her. She had shown up at one of my parties, arms entwined with a good friend of mine. She was his sister, as it had turned out.

As soon as my eyes fell upon her, I knew that I wanted to be hers. I approached her and we soon separated ourselves from the party to a little corner of my home. There we talked far past the time the party had died off. Past even morning, if I recollect correctly.

And so, in the town square - for I had steadfastly refused her plea of a church wedding - we were performing our nuptials. It was this day of my life that I hold the most fondness for. Such a happy time.

Many of the townspeople had shown up. The gift table was filled past capacity as our attendees had been very generous.

There was one gift, though, that nobody claimed as having been theirs. An envelope, manila in color. No name was on it and blank looks were the only response received when the crowd was inquired about it.

Inside, I found two tickets on a well-reputed cruise liner to the Spanish coast. A brief letter accompanied the tickets, saying simply "Happy Honeymoon".

I puzzled over this before turning the letter to find more scrawl on the back. A crudely drawn map to a pier with instructions to ask for a ride to a place called Innsmouth. No name was given for a particular ferry company, nor any further instruction beyond that. Just the promise that our ferry had already been paid for and that a villa awaited us upon our arrival.

A week later and we embarked on our luxury ship to cross the Atlantic. The cruise was nothing short of spectacular. We wanted not for wine, nor song. An absolute pleasure.

Once debarked upon the Spanish coast, we followed the rough map until we were reasonably sure that we had arrived at the indicated pier. Several small boats were tied along it and we had to ask many mariners for passage to Innsmouth. Few spoke English and your mother and I spoke no Spanish at all. The few that spoke our tongue indicated that no such place existed.

We stood baffled until a strange, little man approached us, saying that he knew of Innsmouth and could take us there. We followed him to his boat. It was a meager vessel with the name *Shadow* painted in fading letters across its side.

I stepped onto the boat first, intending to help Sarah bring the bags onboard. As soon as I stepped onto the creaky, wooden deck, a voice whispered in my ear.

It was Silas' voice.

Silas, of course, was nowhere to be found, but I heard his voice just the same.

"Leave, Winny! Leave now!" the whisper warned.

I hadn't seen Silas since nearly ten years after the war had ended. Since then, I am not proud to admit, my thoughts had rarely strayed to him. The sound of his voice on that boat, however, brought back the last encounter that I had with him. He had stopped by the place I was renting at the time and told me that he had discovered something interesting.

You see, since our encounter with the chaplain, Silas had been driven mad with desire to understand what had really happened. That, and he hoped to find the chaplain, who we were sure wasn't really dead. He wanted nothing more than to keep his promise of forever guarding the demon's headless corpse at the point of a shotgun. The desire had burned at him like maddening fever.

Anyway, on that day those many years ago, he had informed me that he had found a promising lead and was going off to investigate it.

He had departed for the Spanish coast the very next day. The very same place your mother and I found ourselves now. I had never seen, nor heard, from Silas again.

Until now.

I looked at the diminutive mariner and apologized to him before hopping back to the pier. Sarah was confused by my actions, but did her best to play along after seeing the look on my face.

The mariner looked briefly perturbed, but didn't try to fight our departure.

"Innsmouth isn't going anywhere. In case you ever change your mind," was the only resistance that he offered.

As I turned from him, in the corner of my eye, I could have sworn that I saw three slits flaring on either side of his neck.

Gills…like those on Olmstead.

When I turned back to him, however, they were gone. Just a normal, if somewhat pallid, neck stood atop his shoulders.

I quickly snatched up the bags and we spent the rest of the trip in a nice room right by the sea. Sarah only ever asked me once what had happened at the boat to suddenly change my mind. I shrugged her question off, because I knew I couldn't answer with the truth. The truth that I knew deep in my gut.

The only thing that would have awaited us in Innsmouth…

…was death.

August 23rd, 1893

And that leads us back to today.

I can hear their horses approaching now. It won't be long before they are here to take me forever away to the asylum.

I plan on going with them peacefully. Part of me even thinks that the asylum may be the best place for me now. The safest place for everyone involved.

You see, three weeks ago, all that I have accomplished these last ten years came unraveled.

The nightmares have returned. The paranoia. The constant state of dread.

And it's all because of him.

The chaplain.

He finally found me. After thirty long years, he has returned.

It was in the market where I saw at last saw him again. Your mother was home caring for you, while I, per her instruction, was out perusing the local produce.

"Hello again, boy."

The voice sent shivers barging down my spine. I had recognized his menacing tone before even the first syllable had left his lips.

The melon in my hand fell loose, bursting apart on the ground. I could hear an irate shopkeeper yelling at me in the background, but his words were lost on me. All my attention was on the scarred façade of the man who stood staring at me with that wicked grin of his.

"I must admit that I was disappointed when I heard that you had declined my wedding gift. Or, at least, the ferry ride to Innsmouth. I was there, you know. In that island village; waiting patiently for your arrival."

I gulped, feeling like a helpless child again. I was unable to speak or otherwise respond. I wanted more than anything to turn and run, but I could not.

"Anyway, I have finally figured out your purpose. It took me many years to ascertain it, but, with the birth of your son, it all became clear. In your blood, lies prophecy."

"My son?" my voice finally cracked. Suddenly, thinking of you, I snapped out of my stupor. My feet were still planted, but my anger allowed my words to burst forth. "Don't you touch him! Not ever!" I shouted. Several head turned towards us, but they didn't linger.

"Do not worry yourself. That is not mine, nor God's, intention for him," the chaplain said soothingly. He then slowly approached me, patting my cheek. When his cold flesh fell on mine, I felt a spark burst in my head. With the spark, the return of all that the Necronomicon had taken from me. "Take care, boy. Have a good life."

Then he walked away, but not before menacingly adding: "What's left of it, anyway."

Since that day, I have fallen apart. To the point that your mother has found no other choice but to have me committed. Do not blame her, though. She has good cause.

Twice now, I am ashamed to admit, I have struck your mother. Not due to intention, but because she startled me from one of the nasty day terrors I have increasingly found myself lost in.

She has been waking during the night, only to find me staring blankly at a wall; sweat staining my bedclothes.

Even small things have been adding up. Things such as sitting together for meals. I will leave my plate mostly untouched and then burst into anger when she challenges me on it.

Finally, last evening she asked me the question that I had been fearing since the market.

Been fearing my whole adult life.

"What is going on, Winfield? Have you gone mad?" she asked. Not with anger, but with utter anguish and hopelessness. My heart broke as I saw the tears soaking her rosy cheeks.

After four years of marriage and five years of our relationship as a whole, I felt that I could tell her my story. Even that I *should* tell her my story. Nobody stood to be affected more than her by the curse that had been returned to me.

So I did. Every last part that I have laid out to you in these pages.

Unfortunately, my tale proved to be too much for her to handle. When I awoke this morning, she had a kitchen knife clutched in her hand. She warned me to stay away from her and informed me of what she had planned. At first, I was angry with her. Furious, even. But now, after having had time to calm myself by writing these words, I understand. It is the only choice she feels that she has. The only choice anybody with a rational mind would feel that they had.

So, she did what she felt she had to do. That is all...no more, no less. Leave her be on the matter and love her always. She will need you now more than ever.

Ha! They have arrived. I have just heard them come crashing through our door. So, I leave you with this:

Heed the warning that I have laid out here for you. I have written this so that you will know the evils that are out there and that you may steer clear from them. Please, I implore you, do not seek these evils out, for I fear that is what the chaplain has in mind. If you ever see the man with the scarred face, RUN!

Do not seek answers beyond what I have laid out for you in these pages. I fear that any such quest will garner the chaplain's attention and bring him intruding into your life. A most unwelcome intrusion, I assure you.

And, lastly, never repeat these words to anybody. Even those closest to you will never believe. They will accuse you of fantasy. Of madness. At best, they will ostracize you from society. At worst, they will have you committed to live out your life with your father in some dark, dour asylum.

Take care, my son. Know that I love you and would do anything for you. You will always be in my thoughts, Howard Phillips. Always.

Sincerely,

Winfield Lovecraft

AFTERWORD

By now I assume that you have come to the conclusion that *Chaplain* is my homage to the incredible H.P. Lovecraft and the great works that he created. I have always been a huge fan of Lovecraft's work and his ideas have inspired me throughout the years on everything from short stories, school projects (admittedly, *that* was a long time ago), and little homemade films that I would make with my friends.

Lovecraft's works have inspired many, many artists over the last century. Many movies, books, and even video games have been steeped in his mythology. And, of course, Lovecraft's influence is heavily evident in my choice of musical genre, Heavy Metal.

There is a sect of people out there that believe that Lovecraft was onto something far more than entertainment value with his works. People believe his creations - such as the Necronomicon and the Ancient Ones - are real, and that Lovecraft was simply trying to warn us of what is out there. Additionally, that he did it through means of stories published in popular fiction journals, where such outlandish tales had a higher chance of reaching the masses. After all, nobody would be interested in reading the ravings of a mad man; at least not back in those days. Our hunger for the sick and twisted has skyrocketed in the last half-century, so who knows how he would approach this in modern times.

Anyway, what if Lovecraft indeed did know more than he was letting on? What if his mythological creations were more than just mythology? I figured it'd be a fun exercise to hypothesize how Lovecraft would come to know of this other world, populated by beasts such as Cthulhu. And Chaplain is the result of that exercise. I hope you enjoyed the story and I look forward to adding more to your library soon.

-Dave

Read on for an excerpt from David W Coons Jr's first
full-length novel

SIXTEEN YEARS AGO

COMING SOON

SIXTEEN YEARS AGO

The noise was deafening – the sight beautiful; but the boss knew it to be deadly as well. It was deadly due to the devastating effect it would have on the body were you to succumb to gravity's embrace. It was easily a couple hundred feet down…and that was just to the treetops. The boss also knew there were plenty of other lethal surprises awaiting below if you *were* to survive the long fall into the never-ending canopy.

Due to the ingenuity of mankind, the boss wasn't concerned about the long drop. For the time being, he was safely tucked away in the belly of the roaring beast. When the time arrived to traverse the span separating him from the ground below, his plunge would be done in a controlled fashion. The phrase *terminal velocity* need not apply.

He smiled while watching the emerald carpet rush by at an incredible pace. It was almost a shame to not be able to linger in admiration of nature's grandeur; but, alas, there was work to be done and time was flying by even faster than the treetops below.

"We'll be arriving at your coordinates in ninety seconds, boss" the man who had commissioned this expedition heard the helicopter pilot say through the headset tightly hugging his ears. "You may want to start getting strapped in."

"You don't have to keep calling me 'boss'? I have a perfectly good name, you know."

Gino was tucked out of sight in the cockpit, but the boss could sense him shrugging just the same.

"Nah…you're the boss, boss. Proper courtesy and such."

The boss shook his head in defeat - his lips curling into a smile.

"Copy all, Gino…hooking up now!" Though the microphone was less than an inch from his lips, the boss had to shout to be heard over the thundering whir of the chopper's engine.

The boss extracted the nylon rope from its bag on the deck, found the end with the steel clip and secured it to a piece known as the donut ring; a round steel structure that was permanently attached to the helicopter's frame. He took the other end of the rope and fed it through his harness, making sure that it was properly seated in the descender he would be using to control the speed of his drop. He finished this part of the ritual by preparing the deployment bag containing his gear. The bag had the added benefit of acting as an anchor to keep the nylon cord weighed down to assist with his descent.

He was just finishing securing the deployment bag to the free end of the rope, when the pilot's voice shot through his earpiece again.

"Sixty seconds, sir."

"Sixty seconds, copy," the boss repeated before turning to the two other men who would be rappelling with him.

"Let's go over this one last time. We're going to touch down at the coordinates of the clearing we identified from the satellite feed. It is only about ten feet in diameter, but it is the only such clearing for forty miles. It lies about one kilometer due east of our objective, so I hope that you're all ready for a bit of a hike."

The boss turned his attention back to the cockpit. "Gino, as soon as we're down, haul up the rope and book ass back to Nauta to refuel. We will call you on the SAT phone when we're readying for extraction."

"Roger that, boss. Thirty seconds, by the way."

"Thirty seconds, aye." The boss nodded to his two partners, emphasizing that it was almost showtime. "Just make sure that you are standing by for that call, Gino. I'd prefer not to spend the night out here."

"Copy that, sir. Will do."

"Alright...Cedric, Chief, you ready?"

Clayton Evans – who liked to be called by his former military rank, Chief - was a hulk of a man, acting as a personal bodyguard for this mission. He nodded enthusiastically at the idea. "It's about damn time we get some action on this little shindig!"

The other adventurer, Cedric Levy, looked far less adventur*ous*. He was shaking; presumably at the prospect of lowering himself from a perfectly good helicopter into one of the most dangerous environs on Earth. He nodded his assent though, knowing that he had no choice in the matter. This task had to be done and he was the only one who could do it.

"Good enough," the boss judged. "Be ready to go as soon as we are set."

"Five seconds, sir," the pilot informed.

SIXTEEN YEARS AGO

"Alright...let's get down there before somebody comes to say hello." The boss opened the chopper's bay door. The fierce wind from the rotor's draft immediately pushed through and flooded the helo.

"Over top, sir," the pilot's voice rang through the speaker.

"Roger, Gino. We'll hopefully see you in a few hours." With that, the boss crouched with his back to the open space and kicked out into the air. He felt the rush as he fell towards the treetops below. He judged that he had covered roughly half the distance before he applied pressure to his descender to slow his plunge. He eased off the device for another drop until he was even with the top of the tree line. He repeated the steps of releasing and trapping the line for the next hundred feet until his feet were firmly planted on the soil of the rainforest.

He hurriedly disconnected his harness from the nylon rope and gave a thumbs up towards the helicopter. Soon after, he saw Cedric dropping towards him. The day prior had seen Cedric's first – and only – rappel, which had been done as practice for today. His drop wasn't very graceful – he nervously came to a stop several times on the way down, his body helplessly flailing while suspended– but he finally touched down next to the boss, seeming none the worse for wear.

"If you'll excuse me, I think I'm going to go over and puke behind that tree now," Cedric notified the boss after removing his harness from the line.

"Stay close...you wouldn't want to be gobbled up by an anaconda or something," he teased with a smile on his face.

The troubled look on Cedric's face indicated that he hadn't recognized the boss' jest as the good-natured joke it was intended to be. He swallowed down any bile that may have been rising in his throat and announced that he had changed his mind.

Clayton, in stark contrast to Cedric, shot damn near to the ground before he finally applied pressure on the descender and slowed himself. He wasn't more than twenty feet over head when he finally stopped.

"Whoo-hoo!" He shouted as he let his grip loosen to finish his descent. "Reminds me of fucking Afghanistan!" After taking a moment to survey the surrounding foliage, he amended the statement. "Quite a bit greener though, I reckon."

Clayton had been a Navy SEAL as recently as the year before...one of the main reasons that the boss had hired him. If you had the money to buy some personal security, you could definitely do worse than a former SEAL.

"Well, Chief, this place is a hell of a lot more deadly than *that* hellhole," the boss stated. "Welcome to the Amazon."

******

A kilometer didn't sound like a great distance – Clayton in particular could have ran a kilometer in just under three minutes on a flat, open road – but when you were battling through some of thickest bush in the world, it could be a long and grueling trek. As it was, the trio had been at it nearly two hours and still had not managed to reach their destination.

"I take back my earlier sentiments...this place sure as fuck ain't Afghanistan," Clayton grumbled.

"True that, Chief...definitely not," the boss confirmed. He reached forward and patted the shoulder nearest him. "How you holding up, Cedric?"

"I've been better. This place is hot, muggy, and I swear I've swatted enough bugs to fill Grand Central Station."

Cedric apparently wasn't enjoying their little trip to paradise.

"I can't even begin to count how many times I've been bitten so far. I'm probably going to wind up with dengue fever...or some other disease that we haven't even discovered yet."

The boss laughed. "Oh come on, Cedric...it isn't *that* bad. We've got to be damn close by now. We'll take care of business and then be out of here to some hot ladies and cold margaritas...at my private island resort, I might add."

Cedric nodded with all of the enthusiasm he could muster – which wasn't much. "Yeah...I guess. That is if we even find what we are looking for out here. I'm not getting a good sense about this place."

"Yeah...neither am I," the boss agreed under his breath.

The group continued through the thick growth, continually stopping to chop away branches, bush, and all manner of other things that were a hindrance to their progress. Luckily they had not come across any creatures large enough to cause any serious damage, and the boss silently thanked the possible celestial entities for that. He had been joking about the anacondas, but he knew that there was a very real possibility of coming across one – or something even worse.

Another ten minutes passed when they started being assaulted by the fragrance of putridity. The forest floor was highly odiferous on its own – every step brought with it a squish from the hefty amount of rotting flora – but this new odor was easily detectable even amongst that. It started off small – just a minor annoyance really- but it quickly escalated into a powerful stench that assailed their nasal cavities.

"Jesus...what is that awful smell?" Cedric asked his jungle mates.

It was Clayton that answered – his tone as grim as the boss had ever heard. "*That* is the smell of rotting bodies...and a lot of them, judging by the intensity of it."

"Oh," was the only response that Cedric gave.

"I couldn't have said it better myself, Cedric," the boss agreed, for lack of a better evaluation.

It took another five minutes of chopping before they came across the first body that sourced the appalling aroma. Actually, body *parts* would be a more accurate description of their discovery.

The boss was lost in the vision before him – enough so that he barely noticed the emphatic heaving behind him as Cedric barfed up the remnants of the MREs the group had eaten shortly after takeoff from Nauta.

"Well, I'll be fucked sideways," Clayton uttered, apparently never having come across anything quite as grotesque in the Taliban-controlled mountain ranges.

"Yep," the boss concurred.

The image that was burning itself into their retinas could be described as a scarecrow...or at least that was the closest comparison that the boss could draw. It was an upright figure consisting of sticks from the surrounding trees connecting several segments of rotting flesh. Two evenly spaced feet gave way to twigs that, in turn, gave way to disjointed knee caps. As the eyes traveled up the figure, more twigs, then a chunk that included the hips, ass, and penis of whatever individual was unlucky enough to have acted as the supplier of this particularly nasty effigy. A woven web of wood snaked up to a strip of flesh making up the chest and shoulders. Two sticks extended out from the sides, leading to severed elbow joints and then, eventually, the hands. One stick acted as a neck, holding up the man's severed head in its entirety, minus the eyes. Concluding the motif's horrificness, carefully placed in the vacated ocular cavities were the severed heads of two Amazonian tree boas – their forked tongues both hanging from their mouths,.

"What are those blue things crawling on it?" Cedric asked, once he had finished vomiting.

"Coprophanaeus lancifer," the boss answered, having also noticed the several large, metallic-blue beetles tearing away at the desiccated flesh. "Also known as the Amazonian scarab beetle. They're eaters of the dead."

"And I have a feeling that they won't be the only ones that we will be coming across," Clayton offered. "I'd say that whoever put this here did so as a warning."

The boss nodded his head. "That and – if I had to guess – to satisfy a sick sense of humor."

"I'd like to meet the sick fuck that finds this amusing...if only to see if he is still laughing when I put a bullet between his eyes."

"Hopefully you'll get your wish, Chief," the boss replied.

The trio continued past the grisly scene, careful to keep their distance from the decaying figure. With every step, the smell of decomposition increased, and they knew that they were closing in on their target.

"There!" Clayton erupted, pointing slightly to the right of their trail. "I see something through the trees."

The boss followed Clayton's gesture and saw it too. It was initially hard to distinguish from the foliage they had been ceaselessly cutting through – as it was made of the very same material – but, with some discernment, the fact that it was a man-made structure became obvious.

"Bingo," the boss celebrated at seeing the tribal hut. "Alright, gentlemen, we have arrived at the village. It's time to find out what awaits us."

SIXTEEN YEARS AGO

✶✶✶✶✶✶

The group quickly discovered that what awaited them was death...and lots of it. The entire village had been left in ruin; the villagers more so than the village itself. Bodies strewn everywhere – not the ideal scenario for somebody with a weak constitution, such as Cedric, who once again found himself vomiting in the nearby vegetation.

"Jesus Christ Almighty...what in the holy hell happened here?" Clayton asked nobody in particular.

The boss estimated that the population of this isolated village had been around one-hundred fifty people; judging by a rough count of the rotting lumps of flesh that were scattered about. Being one of the many hidden tribes of the Amazon, very little was known about these people. The boss' research into them prior to this journey had turned up only two articles that had any mention of them at all – certainly nothing as specific as a census.

"Unfortunately, I think I could answer that question," the boss vaguely implied.

Many of the bodies showed only minor decomposition, suggesting that they had only been dead for a couple days at most. A few, however, looked to have been dead a much longer period of time.

Sorting through the various remains, the boss discovered one body that looked worse off than the others.

"Chief, what do you make of this?" the boss asked, poking the body with a branch that he had obtained from a nearby tree.

Clayton walked over and examined the find. "I couldn't begin to tell you, boss," he exclaimed, admitting the discovery was far outside his knowledge of the world.

The body contained a gaping hole in its chest that looked as if it had been there for a long while. The blood on the corpse's mouth looked far fresher, however – as did the gnawed limb in its grasp.

"If I had to guess, I'd say that this guy has been dead for a month...maybe two. Do you think that this could be a staged scene similar to the scarecrow back there?" Clayton gestured back along the trail they had recently created.

"It's possible, but I doubt it," the boss replied.

"That's reassuring," Clayton muttered as he departed towards a hut that had a makeshift lock securing a thatched door.

"What about this?" Clayton gestured towards the lock, which was just a vine snaked through one edge of the door and into the wall of the doorframe.

"I don't know, but it's worth checking out, wouldn't you say?" The boss smiled at Clayton as he used his machete to slice through the vine. After a quick check on Cedric - who had regained his composure and was approaching them - he pushed the door open and they both walked inside the previously-secured hut.

Instantly they were assaulted by a richer version of the pungent odor they had first discovered as they neared the village. A vast amount of insects were buzzing around inside of the hut...all of which assured there were more bodies to be found inside.

Sure enough, after only a few short steps, the party discovered the carnage within. Ten bodies – now mostly just writhing masses of Amazonian army ants – were lined up on the ground near the left wall. The boss cautiously approached the bodies and saw that their heads – or what remained of them anyway – all hung over a trench that had been dug into the dirt. The heads all had the top of their skulls removed and the brains excised from the bony cavern.

"Oh God...I'm going to barf again," the boss heard behind him. Cedric had finally arrived in the hut, but - by the time the boss had turned around - he saw that he had just as quickly departed back to the undergrowth.

"You picked a helluva soldier there, boss," Clayton commented.

"It's not like I had a lot of options. I'm sure he'll come through when we need him to."

It was then that the boss noticed another door built into the opposite wall.

"It looks like we have another room in here to check out," the boss noted, gesturing towards the door.

Clayton pushed through the door into the room, which strangely resembled a home office – albeit a home office put together quickly, using twigs and vines as its primary building materials. The first thing the boss noticed were several maps and diagrams hanging on the walls. The room also contained a strange centerpiece – a roughly-constructed desk that appeared to have been fashioned out of bone. Not human this time, though – some other denizen of the forest; most likely of the four-legged variety.

On the desk was something that had no business being in the middle of a rainforest – especially this deep in the largest rainforest in the world. The boss grabbed the object off of the desk and studied it. It wasn't until his eyes reached the bottom that he understood its true significance.

"Holy shit!" he exclaimed, causing Clayton to startle.

"What is it, boss?"

The boss looked over at Clayton, his eyes taking on a grim disposition.

"Get outside and call Gino. Tell him that we need extraction ASAP, as well as a booking on the first flight back to America," the boss ordered.

"I think something very bad is about to happen."